THE UNDYING FIRE

By

H. G. WELLS

British Library Cataloguing-in-Publication Data
A catalogue record for this book is available from
the British Library

TO
ALL SCHOOLMASTERS
AND SCHOOLMISTRESSES
AND EVERY TEACHER IN THE WORLD

CONTENTS

H. G. Wells

Herbert George Wells was born in Bromley, England in 1866. He apprenticed as a draper before becoming a pupil-teacher at Midhurst Grammar School in West Sussex. Some years later, Wells won a scholarship to the School of Science in London, where he developed a strong interest in biology and evolution, founding and editing the *Science Schools Journal*. However, he left before graduating to return to teaching, and began to focus increasingly on writing. His first major essay on science, 'The Rediscovery of the Unique', appeared in 1891. However, it was in 1895 that Wells seriously established himself as a writer, with the publication of the now iconic novel, *The Time Machine*.

Wells followed *The Time Machine* with the equally well-received *War of the Worlds* (1898), which proved highly popular in the USA, and was serialized in the magazine *Cosmopolitan*. Around the turn of the century, he also began to write extensively on politics, technology and the future, producing works *The Discovery of the Future* (1902) and *Mankind in the Making* (1903). An active socialist, in 1904 Wells joined the Fabian Society, and his 1905 book *A Modern Utopia* presented a vision of a socialist society founded on reason and compassion. Wells also penned a range of successful comic novels, such as *Kipps* (1905) and *The History of Mr Polly* (1910).

Wells' 1920 work, *The Outline of History,* was penned in response to the Russian Revolution, and declared that world would be improved by education, rather than revolution. It made Wells one of the most important political thinkers of the twenties and thirties, and he began to write for a number of journals and newspapers, even travelling to Russia to lecture Lenin and Trotsky on social reform. Appalled by the carnage of World War II, Wells began to work on a project dealing with the perils of nuclear war, but died before completing it. He is now regarded as one of the greatest science-fiction writers of all time, and an important political thinker.

I. — THE PROLOGUE IN HEAVEN

§ 1

Two eternal beings, magnificently enhaloed, the one in a blinding excess of white radiance and the other in a bewildering extravagance of colours, converse amidst stupendous surroundings. These surroundings are by tradition palatial, but there is now also a marked cosmic tendency about them. They have no definite locality; they are above and comprehensive of the material universe.

There is a quality in the scene as if a futurist with a considerable knowledge of modern chemical and physical speculation and some obscure theological animus had repainted the designs of a pre-Raphaelite. The vast pillars vanish into unfathomable darknesses, and the complicated curves and whorls of the decorations seem to have been traced by the flight of elemental particles. Suns and planets spin and glitter through the avanturine depths of a floor of crystalline ether. Great winged shapes are in attendance, wrought of iridescences and bearing globes, stars, rolls of the law, flaming swords, and similar symbols. The voices of the Cherubim and Seraphim can be heard crying continually, "Holy, Holy, Holy."

Now, as in the ancient story, it is a reception of the sons of God.

The Master of the gathering, to whom one might reasonably

attribute a sublime boredom, seeing that everything that can possibly happen is necessarily known to him, displays on the contrary as lively an interest in his interlocutor as ever. This interlocutor is of course Satan, the Unexpected.

The contrast of these two eternal beings is very marked; while the Deity, veiled and almost hidden in light, with his hair like wool and his eyes like the blue of infinite space, conveys an effect of stable, remote, and mountainous grandeur, Satan has the compact alertness of habitual travel; he is as definite as a grip-sack, and he brings a flavour of initiative and even bustle upon a scene that would otherwise be one of serene perfection. His halo even has a slightly travelled look. He has been going to and fro in the earth and walking up and down in it; his labels are still upon him. His status in heaven remains as undefined as it was in the time of Job; it is uncertain to this day whether he is to be regarded as one of the sons of God or as an inexplicable intruder among them. (But see upon this question the Encyclopaedia Biblica under his name.) Whatever his origin there can be little doubt of his increasing assurance of independence and importance in the Divine presence. His freedom may be sanctioned or innate, but he himself has no doubt remaining of the security of his personal autonomy. He believes that he is a necessary accessory to God, and that his incalculable quality is an indispensable relief to the acquiescences of the Archangels. He never misses these reunions. If God is omnipresent by a calm necessity, Satan is everywhere by an infinite activity. They engage in unending metaphysical differences into which Satan has imported a tone of friendly badinage. They play chess together.

But the chess they play is not the little ingenious game that originated in India; it is on an altogether different scale. The Ruler of the Universe creates the board, the pieces, and the rules; he makes all the moves; he may make as many moves as he likes whenever he likes; his antagonist, however, is permitted to introduce a slight inexplicable inaccuracy into each move, which necessitates further moves in correction. The Creator determines and conceals the aim of the game, and it is never clear whether the purpose of the adversary is to defeat or assist him in his unfathomable project. Apparently the adversary cannot win, but also he cannot lose so long as he can keep the game going. But he is concerned, it would seem, in preventing the development of any reasoned scheme in the game.

§2

Celestial badinage is at once too high and broad to come readily within the compass of earthly print and understanding. The Satanic element of unexpectedness can fill the whole sphere of Being with laughter; thrills begotten of those vast reverberations startle our poor wits at the strangest moments. It is the humour of Satan to thrust upon the Master his own title of the Unique and to seek to wrest from him the authorship of life. (But such jesting distresses the angels.)

"I alone create."

"But I—I ferment."

"Matter I made and all things."

"Stagnant as a sleeping top but for the wabble I give it."

"You are just the little difference of the individual. You are the little Uniqueness in everyone and everything, the Unique that breaks the law, a marginal idiosyncracy."

"Sire, you are the Unique, the Uniqueness of the whole."

Heaven smiled, and there were halcyon days in the planets. "
I shall average you out in the end and you will disappear."

"And everything will end."

"Will be complete."

"Without me!"

"You spoil the symmetry of my universe."

"I give it life."

"Life comes from me."

"No, Sire, life comes from me."

One of the great shapes in attendance became distinct as Michael bearing his sword. " He blasphemes, Lord. Shall I cast him forth?"

"But you did that some time ago," answered Satan, speaking carelessly over his shoulder and not even looking at the speaker. " You keep on doing it. And— I am here."

"He returns," said the Lord soothingly. "Perhaps I will him to return. What should we be without him?"

"Without me, time and space would freeze into crystalline perfection," said Satan, and at his smile the criminal statistics of a myriad planets displayed an upward wave. "It is I who trouble the waters. I trouble all things. I am the spirit of life."

"But the soul," said God.

Satan, sitting with one arm thrown over the back of his throne towards Michael, raised his eyebrows by way of answer. This talk about the soul he regarded as a divine weakness. He knew nothing of the soul.

"I made man in my own image," said God.

"And I made him a man of the world. If it had not been

for me he would still be a needless gardener— pretending to cultivate a weedless garden that grew right because it couldn't grow wrong— in'those endless summers the blessed ones see.' Think of it, ye Powers and Dominions! Perfect flowers! Perfect fruits! Never an autumn chill! Never a yellow leaf! Golden leopards, noble lions, carnivores unfulfilled, purring for his caresses amidst the aimless friskings of lambs that would never grow old! Good Lord! How bored he would have been! How bored! Instead of which, did I not launch him on the most marvellous adventures? It was I who gave him history. Up to the very limit of his possibilities. Up to the very limit.... And did not you, Lord, by sending your angels with their flaming swords, approve of what I had done?"

God gave no answer.

"But that reminds me," said Satan unabashed.

§ 3

The great winged shapes drew nearer, for Satan is the celestial raconteur. He alone makes stories.

"There was a certain man in the land of Uz whose name was Job."

"We remember him."

"We had a wager of sorts," said Satan. "It was some time ago."

"The wager was never very distinct— and now that you remind me of it, there is no record of your paying."

"Did I lose or win! The issue was obscured by discussion. How those men did talk! You intervened. There was no decision."

"You lost, Satan," said a great Being of Light who bore a

book. "The wager was whether Job would lose faith in God and curse him. He was afflicted in every way, and particularly by the conversation of his friends. But there remains an undying fire in man."

Satan rested his dark face on his hand, and looked down between his knees through the pellucid floor to that little eddying in the ether which makes our world. "Job," he said, "lives still."

Then after an interval: "The whole earth is now— Job."

Satan delights equally in statistics and in quoting scripture. He leant back in his seat with an expression of quiet satisfaction. "Job," he said, in easy narrative tones, "lived to a great age. After his disagreeable experiences he lived one hundred and forty years. He had again seven sons and three daughters, and he saw his offspring for four generations. So much is classical. These ten children brought him seventy grandchildren, who again prospered generally and had large families. (It was a prolific strain.) And now if we allow three generations to a century, and the reality is rather more than that, and if we take the survival rate as roughly three to a family, and if we agree with your excellent Bishop Usher that Job lived about thirty-five centuries ago, that gives us— How many? Three to the hundred and fifth power?... It is at any rate a sum vastly in excess of the present population of the earth.... You have globes and rolls and swords and stars here; has anyone a slide rule?"

But the computation was brushed aside.

"A thousand years in my sight are but as yesterday when it is past. I will grant what you seek to prove; that Job has become mankind."

14

§ 4

The dark regard of Satan smote down through the quivering universe and left the toiling light waves behind. "See there," he said pointing. "My old friend on his little planet— Adam— Job— Man— like a roast on a spit. It is time we had another wager."

God condescended to look with Satan at mankind, circling between day and night. "Whether he will curse or bless."

"Whether he will even remember God."

"I have given my promise that I will at last restore Adam."

The downcast face smiled faintly.

"These questions change from age to age," said Satan.

"The Whole remains the same."

"The story grows longer in either direction," said Satan, speaking as one who thinks aloud; "past and future unfold together.... When the first atoms jarred I was there, and so conflict was there— and progress. The days of the old story have each expanded to hundreds of millions of years now, and still I am in them all. The sharks and crawling monsters of the early seas, the first things that crept out of the water into the jungle of fronds and stems, the early reptiles, the leaping and flying dragons of the great age of life, the mighty beasts of hoof and horn that came later; they all feared and suffered and were perplexed. At last came this Man of yours, out of the woods, hairy, beetle-browed and blood-stained, peering not too hopefully for that Eden-bower of the ancient story. It wasn't there. There never had been a garden. He had fallen before he arose, and the weeds and thorns are as ancient as the flowers. The Fall goes back in time now beyond man, beyond the world, beyond imagination. The very stars were born in sin....

"If we can still call it sin," mused Satan.

"On a little planet this Thing arises, this red earth, this Adam, this Edomite, this Job. He builds cities, he tills the earth, he catches the lightning and makes a slave of it, he changes the breed of beast and grain. Clever things to do, but still petty things. You say that in some manner he is to come up at last to *this*.... He is too foolish and too weak. His achievements only illuminate his limitations. Look at his little brain boxed up from growth in a skull of bone! Look at his bag of a body full of rags and rudiments, a haggis of diseases! His life is decay.... *Does* he grow? I do not see it. Has he made any perceptible step forward in quality in the last ten thousand years? He quarrels endlessly and aimlessly with himself.... In a little while his planet will cool and freeze."

"In the end he will rule over the stars," said the voice that was above Satan. "My spirit is in him."

Satan shaded his face with his hand from the effulgence about him. He said no more for a time, but sat watching mankind as a boy might sit on the bank of a stream and watch the fry of minnows in the clear water of a shallow.

"Nay," he said at last, "but it is incredible. It is impossible. I have disturbed and afflicted him long enough. I have driven him as far as he can be driven. But now I am moved to pity. Let us end this dispute. It has been interesting, but now— Is it not enough? It grows cruel. He has reached his limit. Let us give him a little peace now, Lord, a little season of sunshine and plenty, and then some painless universal pestilence and so let him die."

"He is immortal and he does but begin."

16

"He is mortal and near his end. At times no doubt he has a certain air that seems to promise understanding and mastery in his world; it is but an air; give me the power to afflict and subdue him but a little, and after a few squeaks of faith and hope he will whine and collapse like any other beast. He will behave like any kindred creature with a smaller brain and a larger jaw; he too is doomed to suffer to no purpose, to struggle by instinct merely to live, to endure for a season and then to pass.... Give me but the power and you shall see his courage snap like a rotten string."

"You may do all that you will to him, only you must not slay him. For my spirit is in him."

"That he will cast out of his own accord—when I have ruined his hopes, mocked his sacrifices, blackened his skies and filled his veins with torture.... But it is too easy to do. Let me just slay him now and end his story. Then let us begin another, a different one, and something more amusing. Let us, for example, put brains— and this Soul of yours— into the ants or the bees or the beavers! Or take up the octopus, already a very tactful and intelligent creature!"

"No; but do as you have said, Satan. For you also are my instrument. Try Man to the uttermost. See if he is indeed no more than a little stir amidst the slime, a fuss in the mud that signifies nothing...."

§ 5

The Satan, his face hidden in shadow, seemed not to hear this, but remained still and intent upon the world of men.

And as that brown figure, with its vast halo like the worn tail of some fiery peacock, brooded high over the realms of being, this that follows happened to a certain man upon the earth.

II. — AT SEA VIEW SUNDERING-ON-SEA

§ 1

IN an uncomfortable armchair of slippery black horsehair, in a mean apartment at Sundering-on-Sea, sat a sick man staring dully out of the window. It was an oppressive day, hot under a leaden sky; there was scarcely a movement in the air save for the dull thudding of the gun practice at Shorehamstow. A multitude of flies crawled and buzzed fitfully about the room, and ever and again some chained-up cur in the neighbourhood gave tongue to its discontent. The window looked out upon a vacant building lot, a waste of scorched grass and rusty rubbish surrounded by a fence of barrel staves and barbed wire. Between the ruinous notice-board of some pre-war building enterprise and the gaunt verandah of a convalescent home, on which the motionless blue forms of two despondent wounded men in deck chairs were visible, came the sea view which justified the name of the house; beyond a wide waste of mud, over which quivered the heat-tormented air, the still anger of the heavens lowered down to meet in a line of hard conspiracy, the steely criminality of the remote deserted sea.

The man in the chair flapped his hand and spoke. "You accursed creature," he said. "Why did God make flies?"

After a long interval he sighed deeply and repeated: *"Why?"*

He made a fitful effort to assume a more comfortable

position, and relapsed at last into his former attitude of brooding despondency.

When presently his landlady came in to lay the table for lunch, an almost imperceptible wincing alone betrayed his sense of the threatening swish and emphasis of her movements. She was manifestly heated by cooking, and a smell of burnt potatoes had drifted in with her appearance. She was a meagre little woman with a resentful manner, glasses pinched her sharp red nose, and as she spread out the grey-white diaper and rapped down the knives and forks in their places she glanced at him darkly as if his inattention aggrieved her. Twice she was moved to speak and did not do so, but at length she could endure his indifference no longer. "Still feeling ill I suppose, Mr. 'Uss?" she said, in the manner of one who knows only too well what the answer will be.

He started at the sound of her voice, and gave her his attention as if with an effort. "I beg your pardon, Mrs. Croome?"

The landlady repeated with acerbity, " I arst if you was still feeling ill, Mr. 'Uss."

He did not look at her when he replied, but glanced towards her out of the corner of his eyes. "Yes," he said. "Yes, I am. I am afraid I am ill." She made a noise of unfriendly confirmation that brought his face round to her. "But mind you, Mrs. Croome, I don't want Mrs. Huss worried about it. She has enough to trouble her just now. Quite enough."

"Misfortunes don't ever come singly," said Mrs. Croome with quiet satisfaction, leaning across the table to brush some spilt salt from off the cloth to the floor. She was not going to make any rash promises about Mrs. Huss.

"We 'ave to bear up with what is put upon us," said Mrs.

Croome. "We 'ave to find strength where strength is to be found."

She stood up and regarded him with pensive malignity. "Very likely all you want is a tonic of some sort. Very likely you've just let yourself go. I shouldn't be surprised."

The sick man gave no welcome to this suggestion.

"If you was to go round to the young doctor at the corner— Barrack isnameis— very likely he'd put you right. Everybody says he's very clever. Not that me and Croome put much faith in doctors. Nor need to. But you 're in a different position."

The man in the chair had been to see the young doctor at the corner twice already, but he did not want to discuss that interview with Mrs. Croome just then. "I must think about it," he said evasively.

"After all it isn't fair to yourself, it isn't fair to others, to sicken— for it might be anythink— without proper advice. Sitting there and doing nothing. Especially in lodgings at this time of year. It isn't, well not what I call considerate."

"Exactly," said Mr. Huss weakly.

"There's homes and hospitals properly equipped."

The sick man nodded his head appreciatively.

"If things are nipped in the bud they're nipped in the bud, otherwise they grow and make trouble."

It was exactly what her hearer was thinking.

Mrs. Croome ducked to the cellarette of a gaunt sideboard and rapped out a whisky bottle, a bottle of lime-juice, and a soda-water syphon upon the table. She surveyed her handiwork with a critical eye. "Cruet," she whispered, and vanished from the room, leaving the door, after a tormenting phase of creaking, to slam by its own weight behind her....

The invalid raised his hand to his forehead and found it wet with perspiration. His hand was trembling violently. "My *God!*" he whispered.

§ 2

This man's name was Job Huss. His father had been called Job before him, and so far as the family tradition extended the eldest son had always been called Job. Four weeks ago he would have been esteemed by most people a conspicuously successful and enviable man, and then had come a swift rush of disaster.

He had been the headmaster of the great modern public school at Woldingstanton in Norfolk, a revived school under the Papermakers' Guild of the City of London; he had given himself without stint to its establishment and he had made a great name in the world for it and for himself. He had been the first English schoolmaster to liberate the modern side from the entanglement of its lower forms with the classical masters; it was the only school in England where Spanish and Russian were honestly taught; his science laboratories were the best school laboratories in Great Britain and perhaps in the world, and his new methods in the teaching of history and politics brought a steady stream of foreign inquirers to Woldingstanton. The hand of the adversary had touched him first just at the end of the summer term. There had been an epidemic of measles in which, through the inexplicable negligence of a trusted nurse, two boys had died. On the afternoon of the second of these deaths an assistant master was killed by an explosion in the chemical laboratory. Then on the very last night of the term came the School House fire, in which two of the younger boys were burnt to death.

Against any single one of these misfortunes Mr. Huss and his school might have maintained an unbroken front, but their quick succession had a very shattering effect. Every circumstance conspired to make these events vividly dreadful to Mr. Huss. He had been the first to come to the help of his chemistry master, who had fallen among some carboys of acid, and though still alive and struggling, was blinded, nearly faceless, and hopelessly mangled. The poor fellow died before he could be extricated. On the night of the fire Mr. Huss strained himself internally and bruised his foot very painfully, and he himself found and carried out the charred body of one of the two little victims from the room in which they had been trapped by the locking of a door during some "last day" ragging. It added an element of exasperating inconvenience to his greater distresses that all his papers and nearly all his personal possessions were burnt.

On the morning after the fire Mr. Huss's solicitor committed suicide. He was an old friend to whom Mr. Huss had entrusted the complete control of the savings that were to secure him and Mrs. Huss a dignified old age. The lawyer was a man of strong political feelings and liberal views, and he had bought roubles to his utmost for Mr. Huss as for himself, in order to demonstrate his confidence in the Russian revolution.

All these things had a quite sufficiently disorganizing effect upon Mr. Huss; upon his wife the impression they made was altogether disastrous. She was a worthy but emotional lady, effusive rather than steadfast. Like the wives of most schoolmasters, she had been habitually preoccupied with matters of domestic management for many years, and her first reaction was in the direction of a bitter economy, mingled with a display of contempt she had never manifested hitherto for her husband's practical ability. Far better would it have been for him, Huss, if she had broken down altogether; she insisted upon directing everything, and doing so with a sort of pitiful vehemence that brooked no contradiction. It was impossible to stay at Woldingstanton through the vacation, in sight of the tragic and blackened ruins of School House, and so she decided upon Sundering-on-Sea because of its nearness and its pre-war reputation for cheapness. There, she announced, her husband must "pull himself together and pick up," and then return to the rebuilding of School House and the rehabilitation of the school. Many formalities had to be gone through before the building could be put in hand, for in those days Britain was at the extremity of her war effort, and labour and material were unobtainable without special permits and great exertion. Sundering-on-Sea was as convenient a place as anywhere from which to write letters, but his idea of going to London to see influential people was resisted by Mrs. Huss on the score of the expense, and overcome when he persisted in it by a storm of tears.

On her arrival at Sundering Mrs. Huss put up at the Railway Hotel for the night, and spent the next morning in a stern visitation of possible lodgings. Something in the unassuming outlook of Sea View attracted her, and after a long dispute she was able to beat down Mrs. Croome's demand from five to four and a half guineas a week. That afternoon some importunate applicant in an extremity of homelessness— for there had been a sudden rush of visitors to Sundering— offered six guineas.

Mrs. Croome tried to call off her first bargain, but Mrs. Huss was obdurate, and thereafter all the intercourse of landlady and her lodgers went to the unspoken refrain of "I get four and a half guineas and I ought to get six." To recoup herself Mrs. Croome attempted to make extra charges for the use of the bathroom, for cooking after five o 'clock, for cleaning Mr. Huss's brown boots with specially bought brown cream instead of blacking, and for the ink used by him in his very voluminous correspondence; upon all of which points there was much argument and bitterness.

But a heavier blow than any they had hitherto experienced was now to fall upon Mr. and Mrs. Huss. Job in the ancient story had seven sons and three daughters, and they were all swept away. This Job was to suffer a sharper thrust; he had but one dear only son, a boy of great promise, who had gone into the Royal Flying Corps. News came that he had been shot down over the German lines.

Unhappily there had been a conflict between Mr. and Mrs. Huss about this boy. Huss had been proud that the youngster should choose the heroic service; Mrs. Huss had done her utmost to prevent his joining it. The poor lady was now ruthless in her anguish. She railed upon him as the murderer of their child. She hoped he was pleased with his handiwork. He could count one more name on his list; he could add it to the roll of honour in the chapel "with the others." Her *baby* boy! This said, she went wailing from the room.

The wretched man sat confounded. That "with the others " cut him to the heart. For the school chapel had a list of V.C.'s, D.C.M.'s and the like, second to none, and it had indeed been a pride to him.

For some days his soul was stunned. He was utterly exhausted and lethargic. He could hardly attend to the most necessary letters. From dignity, hope, and a great sheaf of activities, his life had shrunken abruptly to the compass of this dingy lodging, pervaded by the squabbling of two irrational women; his work in the world was in ruins; he had no strength left in him to struggle against fate. And a vague internal pain crept slowly into his consciousness.

His wife, insane now and cruel with sorrow, tried to put a great quarrel upon him about wearing mourning for their son. He had always disliked and spoken against these pomps of death, but she insisted that whatever callousness he might display she at least must wear black. He might, she said, rest assured that she would spend no more money than the barest decency required; she would buy the cheapest material, and make it up in her bedroom. But black she must have. This resolution led straight to a conflict with Mrs. Croome, who objected to her best bedroom being littered with bits of black stuff, and cancelled the loan of her sewing machine. The mourning should be made, Mrs. Huss insisted, though she had to sew every stitch of it by hand. And the poor distraught lady in her silly parsimony made still deeper trouble for herself by cutting her material in every direction half an inch or more short of the paper pattern. She came almost to a physical tussle with Mrs. Croome because of the state of the carpet and counterpane, and Mrs. Croome did her utmost to drag Mr. Huss into an altercation upon the matter with her husband.

"Croome don't interfere much, but some things he or nobody ain't going to stand, Mr. Huss."

For some days in this battlefield of insatiable grief and

26

petty cruelty, and with a dull pain steadily boring its way to recognition, Mr. Huss forced himself to carry on in a fashion the complex of business necessitated by the school disaster. Then in the night came a dream, as dreams sometimes will, to enlighten him upon his bodily condition. Projecting from his side he saw a hard, white body that sent round, wormlike tentacles into every corner of his being. A number of doctors were struggling to tear this thing away from him. At every effort the pain increased.

He awoke, but the pain throbbed on.

He lay quite still. Upon the heavy darkness he saw the word "Cancer," bright red and glowing— as pain glows....

He argued in the face of invincible conviction. He kept the mood conditional. "If it be so," he said, though he knew that the thing was so. What should he do? There would have to be operations, great expenses, enfeeblement....

Whom could he ask for advice? Who would help him?...

Suppose in the morning he were to take a bathing ticket as if he meant to bathe, and struggle out beyond the mud-flats. He could behave as though cramp had taken him suddenly....

Five minutes of suffocation he would have to force himself through, and then *peace*—endless peace!

"No," he said, with a sudden gust of courage. "I will fight it out to the end."

But his mind was too dull to form plans and physically he was afraid. He would have to find a doctor somehow, and even that little task appalled him.

Then he would have to tell Mrs. Huss....

For a time he lay quite still as if he listened to the alternative swell and diminuendo of his pain.

"Oh! if I had someone to help me!" he whispered, and was overcome by the lonely misery of his position. "If I had someone"!

For years he had never wept, but now tears were wrung from him. He rolled over and buried his face in the pillow and tried to wriggle his body away from that steady gnawing; he fretted as a child might do."

The night about him was as it were a great watching presence that would not help nor answer.

§ 3

Behind the brass plate at the corner which said "Dr. Elihu Barrack" Mr. Huss found a hard, competent young man, who had returned from the war to his practice at Sundering after losing a leg. The mechanical substitute seemed to have taken to him very kindly. He appeared to be both modest and resourceful; his unfavourable diagnosis was all the more convincing because it was tentative and conditional. He knew the very specialist for the case; no less a surgeon than Sir Alpheus Mengo came, it happened, quite frequently to play golf on the Sundering links. It would be easy to arrange for him to examine Mr. Huss in Dr. Barrack's little consulting room, and if an operation had to be performed it could be managed with a minimum of expense in Mr. Huss's own lodgings without any extra charge for mileage and the like.

"Of course," said Mr. Huss, "of course," with a clear vision of Mrs. Croome confronted with the proposal.

Sir Alpheus Mengo came down the next Saturday, and made

a clandestine examination. He decided to operate the following week-end. Mr. Huss was left at his own request to break the news to his wife and to make the necessary arrangements for this use of Mrs. Croome's rooms. But it was two days before he could bring himself to broach the matter.

He sat now listening to the sounds of his wife moving about in the bedroom overhead, and to the muffled crashes that intimated the climax of Mrs. Croome's preparation of the midday meal. He heard her calling upstairs to know whether Mrs. Huss was ready for her to serve up. He was seized with panic as a schoolboy might be who had not prepared his lesson. He tried hastily to frame some introductory phrases, but nothing would come into his mind save terms of disgust and lamentation. The sullen heat of the day mingled in one impression with his pain. He was nauseated by the smell of cooking. He felt it would be impossible to sit up at table and pretend to eat the meal of burnt bacon and potatoes that was all too evidently coming.

It came. Its progress along the passage was announced by a clatter of dishes. The door was opened by a kick. Mrs. Croome put the feast upon the table with something between defence and defiance in her manner. "What else," she seemed to intimate, "could one expect for four and a half guineas a week in the very height of the season? From a woman who could have got six!"

"Your dinner's there," Mrs. Croome called upstairs to Mrs. Huss in tones of studied negligence, and then retired to her own affairs in the kitchen, slamming the door behind her.

The room quivered down to silence, and then Mr. Huss could hear the footsteps of his wife crossing the bedroom and descending the staircase.

Mrs. Huss was a dark, graceful, and rather untidy lady of seven and forty, with the bridling bearing of one who habitually repels implicit accusations. She lifted the lid of the vegetable dish. "I thought I smelt burning," she said. "The woman is impossible."

She stood by her chair, regarding her husband and waiting.

He rose reluctantly, and transferred himself to a seat at table. It had always been her custom to carve. She now prepared to serve him. "No," he said, full of loathing. "I can't eat. I*can't.*"

She put down the tablespoon and fork she had just raised, and regarded him with eyes of dark disapproval.

"It's all we can get," she said.

He shook his head. "It isn't that."

"I don't know what you expect me to get for you here," she complained. "The tradesmen don't know us— and don't care."

"It isn't that. I'm ill."

"It's the heat. We are all ill. Everyone. In such weather as this. It's no excuse for not making an effort, situated as we are."

"I mean I am really ill. I am in pain."

She looked at him as one might look at an unreasonable child. He was constrained to more definite statement.

"I suppose I must tell you sooner or later. I've had to see a doctor."

"Without consulting me"!

"I thought if it turned out to be fancy I needn't bother you."

"But how did you find a doctor?"

"There's a fellow at the corner. Oh! it's no good making a long story of it. I have cancer.... Nothing will do but an operation." Self-pity wrung him. He controlled a violent desire to cry. "I am too ill to eat. I ought to be lying down."

She flopped back in her chair and stared at him as one stares at some hideous monstrosity. "Oh!" she said. "To have cancer now! In these lodgings!"

"I can't *help* it, " he said in accents that were almost a whine. "I didn't choose the time."

"Cancer!" she cried reproachfully. "The horror of it!"

He looked at her for a moment with hate in his heart. He saw under her knitted brows dark and hostile eyes that had once sparkled with affection, he saw a loose mouth with downturned corners that had been proud and pretty, and this mask of dislike was projecting forward upon a neck he had used to call her head-stalk, so like had it seemed to the stem of some pretty flower. She had had lovely shoulders and an impudent humour; and now the skin upon her neck and shoulders had a little loosened, and she was no longer impudent but harsh. Her brows were moist with heat, and her hair more than usually astray. But these things did not increase, they mitigated his antagonism. They did not repel him as defects; they hurt him as wounds received in a common misfortune. Always he had petted and spared and rejoiced in her vanity and weakness, and now as he realized the full extent of her selfish abandonment a protective pity arose in his heart that overcame his physical pain. It was terrible to see how completely her delicacy and tenderness of mind had been broken down. She had neither the strength nor the courage left even for an unselfish thought. And he could not help her; whatever power he had possessed over her mind had gone long ago. His magic had departed.

Latterly he had been thinking very much of her prospects if he were to die. In some ways his death might be a good thing

31

for her. He had an endowment assurance running that would bring in about seven thousand pounds immediately at his death, but which would otherwise involve heavy annual payments for some years. So far, to die would be clear gain. But who would invest this money for her and look after her interests? She was, he knew, very silly about property; suspicious of people she knew intimately, and greedy and credulous with strangers. He had helped to make her incompetent, and he owed it to her to live and protect her if he could. And behind that intimate and immediate reason for living he had a strong sense of work in the world yet to be done by him, and a task in education still incomplete.

He spoke with his chin in his hand and his eyes staring at the dark and distant sea. "An operation," he said, " might cure me."

Her thoughts, it became apparent, had been travelling through some broken and unbeautiful country roughly parallel with the course of his own. "But need there be an operation?" she thought aloud. "Are they ever any good?"

"I could die," he admitted bitterly, and repented as he spoke.

There had been times, he remembered, when she had said and done sweet and gallant things, poor soul! poor broken companion! And now she had fallen into a darkness far greater than his. He had feared that he had hurt her, and then when he saw that she was not hurt, and that she scrutinized his face eagerly as if she weighed the sincerity of his words, his sense of utter loneliness was completed.

Over his mean drama of pain and debasement in its close atmosphere buzzing with flies, it was as if some gigantic and remorseless being watched him as a man of science might hover over some experiment, and marked his life and all his world. "You are alone," this brooding witness counselled, "you are utterly alone. *Curse God and die.*"

It seemed a long time before Mr. Huss answered this imagined voice, and when he answered it he spoke as if he addressed his wife alone.

"No," he said with a sudden decisiveness. "No. I will face that operation.... We are ill and our hearts are faint. Neither for you, dear, nor for me must our story finish in this fashion. No. I shall go on to the end."

"And have your operation here?" "In this house. It is by far the most convenient place, as things are."

"You may die here!"

"Well, I shall die fighting."

"Leaving me here with Mrs. Croome."

His temper broke under her reply. "Leaving you here with Mrs. Croome," he said harshly.

He got up. "I can eat nothing," he repeated, and dropped back sullenly into the horsehair arm-chair.

There was a long silence, and then he heard the little, almost mouselike, movements of his wife as she began her meal. For a while he had forgotten the dull ache within him, but now, glowing and fading and glowing, it made its way back into his consciousness. He was helpless and perplexed; he had not meant to quarrel. He had hurt this poor thing who had been his love and companion; he had bullied her. His clogged brain could think of nothing to set matters right. He stared with dull eyes at a world utterly hateful to him.

III. — THE THREE VISITORS

§ 1

WHILE this unhappy conversation was occurring at Sundering- on-Sea, three men were discussing the case of Mr. Huss very earnestly over a meatless but abundant lunch in the bow window of a club that gives upon the trees and sunshine of Carlton Gardens. Lobster salad engaged them, and the ice in the jug of hock cup clinked very pleasantly as they replenished their glasses.

The host was Sir Eliphaz Burrows, the patentee and manufacturer of those Temanite building blocks which have not only revolutionized the construction of army hutments, but put the whole problem of industrial and rural housing upon an altogether new footing; his guests were Mr. William Dad, formerly the maker of the celebrated Dad and Showhite car de luxe, and now one of the chief contractors for aeroplanes in England; and Mr. Joseph Farr, the head of the technical section of Woldingstanton School. Both the former gentlemen were governors of that foundation and now immensely rich, and Sir Eliphaz had once been a pupil of the father of Mr. Huss and had played a large part in the appointment of the latter to Woldingstanton. He was a slender old man, with an avid vulturine head poised on a long red neck, and he had an abundance of parti-coloured hair, red and white, springing from a circle round the crown of his head, from his eyebrows, his face generally, and the backs of his hands. He wore a blue soft shirt with a turn-down collar within a roomy blue serge suit, and that and something about his large loose black tie suggested scholarship and refinement. His manners were elaborately courteous. Mr. Dad was a compacter, keener type, warily alert in his bearing, an industrial fox-terrier from the Midlands, silver-haired and dressed in ordinary morning dress except for a tan vest with a bright brown ribbon border. Mr. Farr was big in a grey flannel Norfolk suit; he had a large, round, white, shiny, clean-shaven face and uneasy hands, and it was apparent that he carried pocket-books and suchlike luggage in his breast pocket. They consumed the lobster appreciatively, and approached in a fragmentary and tentative manner the business that had assembled them: namely, the misfortunes that had overwhelmed Mr. Huss and their bearing upon the future of the school.

"For my part I don't think there is such a thing as misfortune," said Mr. Dad. "I don't hold with it. Miscalculation *if* you like."

"In a sense," said Mr. Farr ambiguously, glancing at Sir Eliphaz.

"If a man keeps his head screwed on the right way," said Mr. Dad, and attacked a claw with hope and appetite. Mr. Dad affected the parsimony of unfinished sentences.

"I can't help thinking," said Sir Eliphaz, putting down his glass and wiping his moustache and eyebrows with care before resuming his lobster, " that a man who entrusts his affairs to a solicitor, after the fashion of the widow and orphan, must be singularly lacking in judgment. Or reckless. Never in the whole course of my life have I met a solicitor who could invest money safely and profitably. Clergymen I have known, women of all sorts, savages, monomaniacs, criminals, but never solicitors."

"I have known some smart business parsons," said Mr. Dad judicially. "One in particular. Sharp as nails. They are a much underestimated class."

"Perhaps it is natural that a solicitor should be a wild investor," Sir Eliphaz pursued his subject. "He lives out of the ordinary world in a dirty little office in some antiquated inn, his office fittings are fifty years out of date, his habitual scenery consists of tin boxes painted with the names of dead and disreputable clients; he has to take the law courts, filled with horse-boxes and men dressed up in gowns and horse-hair wigs, quite seriously; nobody ever goes near him but abnormal people or people in abnormal states: people upset by jealousy, people upset by fear, blackmailed people, cheats trying to dodge the law, lunatics, litigants and legatees. The only investments he ever discusses are queer investments. Naturally he loses all sense of proportion. Naturally he becomes insanely suspicious; and when a client asks for positive action he flounders and gambles."

"Naturally," said Mr. Dad. "And here we find poor Huss giving all his business over—"

"Exactly," said Sir Eliphaz, and filled his glass.

"There's been a great change in him in the last two years," said Mr. Farr. "He let the war worry him for one thing."

"No good doing that," said Mr. Dad.

"And even before the war," Sir Eliphaz.

"Even before the war," said Mr. Farr, in a pause.

"There was a change," said Sir Eliphaz. "He had been bitten by educational theories."

"No business for a headmaster," said Mr. Farr.

"Our intention had always been a great scientific and technical school," said Sir Eliphaz. "He introduced Logic into the teaching of plain English— against my opinion. He encouraged some of the boys to read philosophy."

"All he could," said Mr. Farr.

"I never held with his fad for teaching history," said Mr. Dad. "He was history mad. It got worse and worse. What's history after all? At the best, it's over and done with.... But he wouldn't argue upon it— not reasonably. He was— overbearing. He had a way of looking at you.... It was never our intention to make Woldingstanton into a school of history."

"And now, Mr. Farr," said Sir Eliphaz, "what are the particulars of the fire?"

"It isn't for me to criticize," said Mr. Farr.

"What I say," said Mr. Dad, projecting his muzzle with an appearance of great determination, " is, fix responsibility. *Fix responsibility.* Here is a door locked that common sense dictated should be open. Who was responsible?"

"No one in School House seems to have been especially responsible for that door so far as I can ascertain," said Mr. Farr.

"All responsibility," said Mr. Dad, with an expression of peevish insistence, as though Mr. Farr had annoyed him, "*all*responsibility that is not delegated rests with the Head. That's a hard and fast and primary rule of business organization. In my factory I say quite plainly to everyone who comes into it, man or woman, chick or child..."

Mr. Dad was still explaining in a series of imaginary dialogues, tersely but dramatically, his methods of delegating authority, when Sir Eliphaz cut across the flow with, " Returning to Mr. Huss for a moment..."

The point that Sir Eliphaz wanted to get at was whether Mr. Huss expected to continue headmaster at Woldingstanton. From some chance phrase in a letter Sir Eliphaz rather gathered that he did.

"Well," said Mr. Farr portentously, letting the thing hang for a moment, "he does."

"Tcha!" said Mr. Dad, and shut his mouth tightly and waved his head slowly from side to side with knitted brows as if he had bitten his tongue.

"I would be the first to recognize the splendid work he did for the school in his opening years," said Mr. Farr. "I would be the last to alter the broad lines of the work as he set it out. Barring that I should replace a certain amount of the biological teaching and practically all this new history stuff by chemistry and physics. But one has to admit that Mr. Huss did not know when to relinquish power nor when to devolve responsibility. We, all of us, the entire staff— it is no mere personal grievance of mine— were kept, well, to say the least of it, in tutelage. Rather than let authority go definitely out of his hands, he would allow things to drift. Witness that door, witness the business of the nurse."

Mr. Dad, with his lips compressed, nodded his head; each nod like the tap of a hammer.

"I never believed in all this overdoing history in the school," Mr. Dad remarked rather disconnectedly. "If you get rid of Latin and Greek, why bring it all back again in another form f Why, I'm told he taught J em things about Assyria. Assyria! A modern school ought to be a modern school business first and business last and business all the time. And teach boys to work. We shall need it, mark my words."

"A certain amount of modern culture," waved Sir Eliphaz.

"*Modern*," said Mr. Farr softly.

Mr. Dad grunted. "In my opinion that sort of thing gives the boys ideas."

Mr. Farr steered his way discreetly. "Science with a due regard to its technical applications should certainly be the substantial part of a modern education."...

They were in the smoking-room and half way through three princely cigars before they got beyond such fragmentary detractions of the fallen headmaster. Then Mr. Dad in the clear-cut style of a business man, brought his companions to action. "Well," said Mr. Dad, turning abruptly upon Sir Eliphaz, " what about it?"

"It is manifest that Woldingstanton has to enter on a new phase; what has happened brings us to the parting of the ways," said Sir Eliphaz. "Much as I regret the misfortunes of an old friend."

"*That,*" said Mr. Dad, "spells Farr."

"If he will shoulder the burthen," said Sir Eliphaz, smiling upon Mr. Farr not so much with his mouth as by the most engaging convolutions, curvatures and waving about of his various strands of hair.

"I don't want to see the school go down," said Mr. Farr. "I've given it a good slice of my life."

"Eight," said Mr. Dad. "Eight. File that. That suits us. And now how do we set about the affair? The next thing, I take it, is to break it to Huss.... How?"

He paused to give the ideas of his companions a fair chance.

"Well, my idea is this. None of us want to be hard on Mr. Huss. Luck has been hard enough as it is. We want to do this job as gently as we can. It happens that I go and play golf at Sundering-on-Sea ever and again. Excellent links, well kept up all things considered, and the big hotel close by does you wonderfully, the railway company sees to that; in spite of the war. Well, why shouldn't we all, if Sir Eliphaz's engagements permit, go down there in a sort of casual way, and take the opportunity of a good clear talk with him and settle it all up? The thing's got to be done, and it seems to me altogether more kindly to go there personally and put it to him than do it by correspondence. Very likely we could put it to him in such a way that he himself would suggest the very arrangement we want. You particularly, Sir Eliphaz, being as you say an old friend."

§ 2

Since there was little likelihood of Mr. Huss going away from Sundering-on-Sea, it did not appear necessary to Mr. Dad to apprise him of the projected visitation. And so these three gentlemen heard nothing about any operation for cancer until they reached that resort.

Mr. Dad came down early on Friday afternoon to the Golf Hotel, where he had already engaged rooms for the party. He needed the relaxation of the links very badly, the task of accumulating a balance sufficiently large to secure an opulent future for British industry, with which Mr. Dad in his straightforward way identified himself, was one that in a controlled establishment between the Scylla of aggressive labour and the Charybdis of the war-profits tax, strained his mind to the utmost. He was joined by Mr. Farr at dinner-time, and Sir Eliphaz, who was detained in London by some negotiations with the American Government, arrived replete by the dining-car train. Mr. Farr made a preliminary reconnaissance at Sea View, and was the first to hear of the operation.

Sir Alpheus Mengo was due at Sea View by the first morning train on Saturday. He had arranged to operate before lunch. It was clear therefore that the only time available for a conversation between the three and Mr. Huss was between breakfast and the arrival of Sir Alpheus.

Mr. Huss, whose lethargy had now departed, displayed himself feverishly anxious to talk about the school. "There are points I must make clear," he said, " vital points," and so a meeting was arranged for half -past nine. This would give a full hour before the arrival of the doctors.

"He feels that in a way it will be his testament, so to speak," said Mr. Farr. "Naturally he has his own ideas about the future of the school. We all have. I would be the last person to suggest that he could say anything about Woldingstanton that would not be well worth hearing. Some of us may have heard most of it before, and be better able to discount some of his assertions. But that under the present circumstances is neither here nor there."

§ 3

Matters in the confined space of Sea View were not nearly so strained as Mr. Huss had feared. The prospect of an operation was not without its agreeable side to Mrs. Croome. Possibly she would have preferred that the subject should have been Mrs. rather than Mr. Huss, but it was clear that she made no claim to dictate upon this point. Her demand for special fees to meet the inconveniences of the occasion had been met quite liberally by Mr. Huss. And there was a genuine appreciation of order and method in Mrs. Croome; she was a furious spring-cleaner, a hurricane tidier-up, her feeling for the discursive state of Mrs. Huss's hair was almost as involuntary as a racial animosity; and the swift dexterous preparations of the nurse who presently came to convert the best bedroom to surgical uses, impressed her deeply. She was allowed to help. Superfluous hangings and furnishings were removed, everything was thoroughly scrubbed, at the last moment clean linen sheets of a wonderful hardness were to be spread over every exposed surface. They were to be brought in sterilized drums. The idea of sterilized drums fascinated her. She had never heard of such things before. She wished she could keep her own linen in a sterilized drum always, and let her lodgers have something else instead.

She felt she was going to be a sort of assistant priestess at a sacrifice, the sacrifice of Mr. Huss. She had always secretly feared his submissive quiet as a thing unaccountable that might at any time turn upon her; she suspected him of ironies; and he would be helpless, under chloroform, subject to examination with no possibilities of disconcerting repartee. She did her best to persuade Dr. Barrack that she would be useful in the room during the proceedings. Her imagination conjured up a wonderful vision of the Huss interior as a great chest full of strange and interesting viscera with the lid wide open and Sir Alpheus picking thoughtfully, with deprecatory remarks, amid its contents. But that sight was denied her.

She was very helpful and cheerful on the Saturday morning, addressing herself to the consolation of Mr. and the bracing-up of Mrs. Huss. She assisted in the final transformation of the room.

"It might be a real 'ospital," she said. "Nursing must be nice work. I never thought of it like this before."

Mr. Huss was no longer depressed but flushed and resolute, but Mrs. Huss, wounded by the neglect of everyone— no one seemed to consider for a moment what she must be feeling— remained very much in her own room, working inefficiently upon the mourning that might now be doubly needed.

§ 4

Mr. Huss knew Mr. Farr very well. For the last ten years it had been his earnest desire to get rid of him, but he had been difficult to replace because of his real accomplishment in technical chemistry. In the course of their five minutes' talk in his bedroom on Friday evening, Mr. Huss grasped the situation. Woldingstanton, his creation, his life work, was to be taken out of his hands, and in favour of this, his most soul-deadening assistant. He had been foolish no doubt, but he had never anticipated that. He had never supposed that Farr would dare.

He thought hard through that long night of Friday. His pain was no distraction. He had his intentions very ready and clear in his mind when his three visitors arrived.

He had insisted upon getting up and dressing fully.

"I can't talk about Woldingstanton in bed," he said. The doctor was not there to gainsay him.

Sir Eliphaz was the first to arrive, and Mrs. Huss retrieved him from Mrs. Croome in the passage and brought him in. He was wearing a Norfolk jacket suit of a coarse yet hairy consistency and of a pale sage green colour. He shone greatly in the eyes of Mrs. Huss. "I can't help thinking of you, dear lady," he said, bowing over her hand, and all his hair was for a moment sad and sympathetic like a sick Skye terrier's. Mr. Dad and Mr. Farr entered a moment later; Mr. Farr in grey flannel trousers and a brown jacket, and Mr. Dad in a natty dark grey suit with a luminous purple waistcoat.

"My dear," said Mr. Huss. to his wife, "I must be alone with these gentlemen," and when she seemed disposed to linger near the understanding warmth of Sir Eliphaz, he added, "Figures, my dear— *Finance*," and drove her forth....

"'Pon my honour," said Mr. Dad, coming close up to the armchair, wrinkling his muzzle and putting through his compliments in good business-like style before coming to the harder stuff in hand; " I don't like to see you like this, Mr. Huss."

"Nor does Sir Eliphaz, I hope— nor Farr. Please find yourselves chairs."

And while Mr. Farr made protesting noises and Sir Eliphaz waved his hair about before beginning the little speech he had prepared, Mr. Huss took the discourse out of their mouths and began:

"I know perfectly well the task you have set yourselves. You have come to make an end of me as headmaster of Woldingstanton. And Mr. Farr has very obligingly..."

He held up his white and wasted hand as Mr. Farr began to disavow.

"No," said Mr. Huss. "But before you three gentlemen proceed with your office, I should like to tell you something of what the school and my work in it, and my work for education, is to me. I am a man of little more than fifty. A month ago I counted with a reasonable confidence upon twenty years more of work before I relaxed.... Then these misfortunes rained upon me. I have lost all my private independence; there have been these shocking deaths in the school; my son, my only son... killed... trouble has darkened the love and kindness of my wife... and now my body is suffering so that my mind is like a swimmer struggling through waves of pain... far from land.... These are heavy blows. But the hardest blow of all, harder to bear than any of these others— I do not speak rashly, gentlemen, I have thought it out through an endless night— the last blow will be this rejection of my life work. That will strike the inmost me, the heart and soul of me...."

He paused.

"You mustn't take it quite like that, Mr. Huss," protested Mr. Dad. "It isn't fair to us to put it like that."

"I want you to listen to me," said Mr. Huss.

"Only the very kindest motives," continued Mr. Dad.

"Let me speak," said Mr. Huss, with the voice of authority that had ruled Woldingstanton for five and twenty years. "I cannot wrangle and contradict. At most we have an hour."

Mr. Dad made much the same sound that a dog will make

when it has proposed to bark and has been told to get under the table. For a time he looked an ill-used man.

"To end my work in the school will be to end me altogether.... I do not see why I should not speak plainly to you, gentlemen, situated as I am here. I do not see why I should not talk to you for once in my own language. Pain and death are our interlocutors; this is a rare and raw and bleeding occasion; in an hour or so the women may be laying out my body and I may be silent for ever. I have hidden my religion, but why should I hide it now? To you I have always tried to seem as practical and self-seeking as possible, but in secret I have been a fanatic; and Woldingstanton was the altar on which I offered myself to God. I have done ill and feebly there I know; I have been indolent and rash; those were my weaknesses; but I have done my best. To the limits of my strength and knowledge I have served God.... And now in this hour of darkness where is this God that I have served? Why does he not stand here between me and this last injury you would do to the work I have dedicated to him?"

At these words Mr. Dad turned horrified eyes to Mr. Farr.

But Mr. Huss went on as though talking to himself. "In the night I have looked into my heart; I have sought in my heart for base motives and secret sins. I have put myself on trial to find why God should hide himself from me now, and I can find no reason and no justification.... In the bitterness of my heart I am tempted to give way to you and to tell you to take the school and to do just what you will with it.... The nearness of death makes the familiar things of experience flimsy and unreal, and far more real to me now is this darkness that broods over me, as blight will sometimes overhang the world at noon, and mocks me day and night with a perpetual challenge to curse God and die....

"Why do I not curse God and die? Why do I cling to my work when the God to whom I dedicated it is— silent? Because, I suppose, I still hope for some sign of reassurance. Because I am not yet altogether defeated. I would go on telling you why I want Woldingstanton to continue on its present lines and why it is impossible for you, why it will be a sort of murder for you to hand it over to Farr here, if my pain were ten times what it is...."

At the mention of his name, Mr. Farr started and looked first at Mr. Dad, and then at Sir Eliphaz. "Really," he said, "really! One might think I had conspired—"

"I am afraid, Mr. Huss," said Sir Eliphaz, with a large reassuring gesture to the technical master, " that the suggestion that Mr. Farr should be your successor came in the first instance from *me*."

"You must reconsider it," said Mr. Huss, moistening his lips and staring steadfastly in front of him.

Here Mr. Dad broke out in a querulous voice: "Are you really in a state, Mr. Huss, to discuss a matter like this— feverish and suffering as you are?"

"I could not be in a better frame for this discussion," said Mr. Huss.... "And now for what I have to say about the school:— Woldingstanton, when I came to it, was a humdrum school of some seventy boys, following a worn-out routine. A little Latin was taught and less Greek, chiefly in order to say that Greek was taught; some scraps of mathematical processes, a few rags of general knowledge, English history— not human history, mind you, but just the national brand, cut dried flowers from the past with no roots and no meaning, a smattering of French.... That was practically all; it was no sort of education, it was a mere education-like posturing. And to-day, what has that school become?"

"We never grudged you money," said Sir Eliphaz.

"Nor loyal help," said Mr. Fair, but in a half whisper.

"I am not thinking of its visible prosperity. The houses and laboratories and museums that have grown about that nucleus are nothing in themselves. The reality of a school is not in buildings and numbers but in matters of the mind and soul. Woldingstanton has become a torch at which lives are set aflame. I have lit a candle there— the winds of fate may yet blow it into a world-wide blaze."

As Mr. Huss said these things he was uplifted by enthusiasm, and his pain sank down out of his consciousness.

"What," he said, " is the task of the teacher in the world? It is the greatest of all human tasks. It is to ensure that Man, Man the Divine, grows in the souls of men. For what is a man without instruction? He is born as the beasts are born, a greedy egotism, a clutching desire, a thing of lusts and fears. He can regard nothing except in relation to himself. Even his love is a bargain; and his utmost effort is vanity because he has to die. And it is we teachers alone who can lift him out of that self-preoccupation. We teachers.... We can release him into a wider circle of ideas beyond himself in which he can at length forget himself and his meagre personal ends altogether. We can open his eyes to the past and to the future and to the undying life of Man. So through us and through us only, he escapes from death and futility. An untaught man is but himself alone, as lonely in his ends and destiny as any beast; a man instructed is a man enlarged from that narrow prison of self into participation in an undying life, that began we know not when, that grows

48

above and beyond the greatness of the stars...."

He spoke as if he addressed some other hearer than the three before him. Mr. Dad, with eyebrows raised and lips compressed, nodded silently to Mr. Farr as if his worst suspicions were confirmed, and there were signs and signals that Sir Eliphaz was about to speak, when Mr. Huss resumed.

"For five and twenty years I have ruled over Woldingstanton, and for all that time I have been giving sight to the blind. I have given understanding to some thousands of boys. All those routines of teaching that had become dead we made live again there. My boys have learnt the history of mankind so that it has become their own adventure; they have learnt geography so that the world is their possession; I have had languages taught to make the past live again in their minds and to be windows upon the souls of alien peoples. Science has played its proper part; it has taken my boys into the secret places of matter and out among the nebulae.... Always I have kept Farr and his utilities in their due subordination. Some of my boys have already made good business-men— because they were more than business-men.... But I have never sought to make business-men and I never will. My boys have gone into the professions, into the services, into the great world and done well I have had dull boys and intractable boys, but nearly all have gone into the world gentlemen, broadminded, good-mannered, understanding and unselfish, masters of self, servants of man, because the whole scheme of their education has been to release them from base and narrow things.... When the war came, my boys were ready.... They have gone to their deaths—how many have gone to their deaths! My own son among them.... I did not grudge him.... Woldingstanton is a new school; its tradition has scarcely begun; the list of its old boys is now so terribly depleted that its young tradition wilts like a torn seedling.... But still we can keep on with it, still that tradition will grow, if my flame still burns. But my teaching must go on as I have planned it. It must. It must.... What has made my boys all that they are, has been the history, the biological science, the philosophy. For these things are wisdom. All the rest is training and mere knowledge. If the school is to live, the head must still be a man who can teach history—history in the widest sense; he must be philosopher, biologist, and archaeologist as well as scholar. And you would hand that task to Farr! Farr! Farr here has never even touched the essential work of the school. He does not know what it is. His mind is no more opened than the cricket professional's."

Mr. Dad made an impatient noise.

The sick man went on with his burning eyes on Farr, his lips bloodless.

"He thinks of chemistry and physics not as a help to understanding but as a help to trading. So long as he has been at Woldingstanton he has been working furtively with our materials in the laboratories, dreaming of some profitable patent. Oh! I know you, Farr. Do you think I didn't see because I didn't choose to complain? If he could have discovered some profitable patent he would have abandoned teaching the day he did so. He would have been even as you are. But with a lifeless imagination you cannot even invent patentable things. He would talk to the boys of the empire at times, but the empire to him is no more than a trading conspiracy fenced about with tariffs. It goes on to nothing.... And he thinks we are fighting the Germans, he thinks my dear and precious boy gave his life and that all these other brave lads beyond counting died, in order that we might take the place of the Germans as the chapman-bullies of the world. That is the measure of his mind. He has no religion, no faith, no devotion. Why does he want my place? Because he wants to serve as I have served? No! But because he envies my house, my income, my headship. Whether I live or die, it is impossible that Woldingstanton, my Woldingstanton, should live under his hand. Give it to him, and in a little while it will be dead."

§ 5

"Gentlemen!" Mr. Fair protested with a white perspiring face.

"I had no idea," ejaculated Mr. Dad, " I had no idea that things had gone so far."

Sir Eliphaz indicated by waving his hand that his associates might allay themselves; he recognized that the time had come for him to speak.

"It is deplorable," Sir Eliphaz began.

He put down his hands and gripped the seat of his chair as if to hold himself on to it very tightly, and he looked very hard at the horizon as if he was trying to decipher some remote inscription. "You have imported a tone into this discussion," he tried.

He got off at the third attempt. "It is an extremely painful thing to me, Mr. Huss, that to you, standing as you do on the very brink of the Great Chasm, it should be necessary to speak in any but the most cordial and helpful tones. But it is my duty, it is our duty, to hold firmly to those principles which have always guided us as governors of the Woldingstanton School. You speak, I must say it, with an extreme arrogance of an institution to which all of us here have in some measure contributed; you speak as though you, and you alone, were its creator and guide. You must pardon me, Mr. Huss, if I remind you of the facts, the eternal verities of the story. The school, sir, was founded in the spacious days of Queen Elizabeth, and many a good man guided its fortunes down to the time when an unfortunate— a diversion of its endowments led to its temporary cessation. The Charity Commissioners revived it after an inquiry some fifty years ago, and it has been largely the lavish generosity of the Papermakers' Guild, of which I and Dad are humble members, that has stimulated its expansion under you. Loth as I am to cross your mood, Mr. Huss, while you are in pain and anxiety, I am bound to recall to you these things which have made your work possible. You could not have made bricks without straw, you could not have built up Woldingstanton without the money obtained by that commercialism for which you display such unqualified contempt. We sordid cits it was who planted, who watered...."

Mr. Huss seemed about to speak, but said nothing.

"Exactly what I say," said Mr. Dad, turning for confirmation to Mr. Farr. "The school is essentially a modern commercial school. It should be run as that."

Mr. Farr nodded his white face ambiguously with his eye on Sir Eliphaz.

"I should have been chary, Mr. Huss, of wrangling about our particular shares and contributions on an occasion so solemn as this, but since you will have it so, since you challenge discussion...."

He turned to his colleagues as if for support.

"Go on, " said Mr. Dad. "Facts are facts."

§ 6

Sir Eliphaz cleared his throat, and continued to read the horizon.

"I have raised these points, Mr. Huss, by way of an opening. The gist of what I have to say lies deeper. So far I have dealt with the things you have said only in relation to us; as against us you assume your own righteousness, you flout our poor judgments, you sweep them aside; the school must be continued on your lines, the teaching must follow your schemes. You can imagine no alternative opinion. God forbid that I should say a word in my own defence; I have given freely both of my time and of my money to our school; it would tax my secretaries now to reckon up how much; but I make no claims.... None....

"But let me now put all this discussion upon a wider and a graver footing. It is not only us and our poor intentions you arraign. Strange things have dropped from you, Mr. Huss, in this discussion, things it has at once pained and astonished me to hear from you. You have spoken not only of man's ingratitude, but of God's. I could scarcely believe my ears, but indeed I heard you say that God was silent, unhelpful, and that he too had deserted you. In spite of the most meritorious exertions on your part.... Standing as you do on the very margin of the Great Secret, I want to plead very earnestly with you against all that you have said."

Sir Eliphaz seemed to meditate remotely. He returned like

a soaring vulture to his victim. "I would be the last man to obtrude my religious feelings upon anyone.... I make no parade of religion, Mr. Huss, none at all. Many people think me no better than an unbeliever. But here I am bound to make my confession. I owe much to God, Mr. Huss...."

He glowered at the sick man. He abandoned his grip upon the seat of his chair for a moment, to make a gesture with his hairy claw of a hand.

"Your attitude to my God is a far deeper offence to me than any merely personal attack could be. Under his chastening blows, under trials that humbler spirits would receive with thankfulness and construe as lessons and warnings, you betray yourself more proud, more self-assured, more— froward is not too harsh a word— more froward, Mr. Huss, than you were even in the days when we used to fret under you on Founder's Day in the Great Hall, when you would dictate to us that here you must have an extension and there you must have a museum or a picture room or what not, leaving nothing to opinion, making our gifts a duty.... You will not recognise the virtue of gifts and graces either in man or God.... Cannot you see, my dear Mr. Huss, the falsity of your position! It is upon that point that I want to talk to you now. God does not smite man needlessly. This world is all one vast intention, and not a sparrow falls to the ground unless He wills that sparrow to fall. Is your heart so sure of itself? Does nothing that has happened suggest to you that there may be something in your conduct and direction of Woldingstanton that has made it not quite so acceptable an offering to God as you have imagined it to be?"

Sir Eliphaz paused with an air of giving Mr. Huss his chance, but meeting with 110 response, he resumed: "I am an old man, Mr. Huss, and I have seen much of the world and more particularly of the world of finance and industry, a world of swift opportunities and sudden temptations. I have watched the careers of many young men of parts, who have seemed to be under the impression that the world had been waiting for them overlong; I have seen more promotions, schemes and enterprises, great or grandiose, than I care to recall. Developing Woldingstanton from the mere endowed school of a market-town it was, to its present position, has been for me a subordinate incident, a holiday task, a piece of by-play upon a crowded scene. My experiences have been on a far greater scale. Far greater. And in all my experience I have never seen what I should call a really right-minded man perish or an innocent dealer— provided, that is, that he took ordinary precautions— destroyed. Ups and downs no doubt there are, for the good as well as the bad. I have seen the foolish taking root for a time—it was but for a time. I have watched the manoeuvres of some exceedingly crafty men."

Sir Eliphaz shook his head slowly from side to side and all the hairs on his head waved about.

He hesitated for a moment, and decided to favour his hearers with a scrap of autobiography.

"Quite recently," he began, "there was a fellow came to us, just as we were laying down our plant for production on a large scale. He was a very plausible, energetic young fellow indeed, an American Armenian. Well, he happened to know somehow that we were going to use kaolin from felspar, a by- product of the new potash process, and he had got hold of a scheme for washing London clay that produced, he assured us, an accessible kaolin just as good for our purpose and not a tenth of the cost of the Norwegian stuff. It would have reduced our prime cost something like thirty per cent. Let alone tonnage. Excuse these technicalities. On the face of it it was a thoroughly good thing. The point was that I knew all along that his stuff retained a certain amount of sulphur and couldn't possibly make a building block to last. That wouldn't prevent us selling and using the stuff with practical impunity. It wasn't up to us to know. No one could have made us liable. The thing indeed looked so plain and safe that I admit it tempted me sorely. And then, Mr. Huss, God came in. I received a secret intimation. I want to tell you of this in all good faith and simplicity. In the night when all the world was deep in sleep, I awoke. And I was in the extremest terror; my very bones were shaking; I sat up in my bed afraid almost to touch the switch of the electric light; my hair stood on end. I could see nothing, I could hear nothing, but it was as if a spirit passed in front of my face. And in spite of the silence something seemed to be saying to me: 'How about God, Sir Eliphaz? Have you at last forgotten Him? How can you, that would dwell in houses of clay, whose foundation is the dust, escape His judgments?' That was all, Mr. Huss, just that. 'Whose foundation is the dust!' Straight to the point. Well, Mr. Huss, I am not a religious man, but I threw over that Armenian."

Mr. Dad made a sound to intimate that he would have done the same.

"I mention this experience, this intervention— and it is not the only one of which I could tell— because I want you to get my view that if an enterprise, even though it is as fair and honest-seeming a business as Woldingstanton School, begins suddenly to crumple and wilt, it means that somehow, somewhere you must have been putting the wrong sort of clay into it. It means not that God is wrong and going back upon you, but that you are wrong. You may be a great and famous teacher now, Mr. Huss, thanks not a little to the pedestal we have made for you, but God is a greater and more famous teacher. He manifestly you have not convinced, even if you could have convinced us, of Woldingstanton's present perfection....

"That is practically all I have to say. When we propose, in all humility, to turn the school about into new and less pretentious courses and you oppose us, that is our answer. If you had done as well and wisely as you declare, you would not be in this position and this discussion would never have arisen."

He paused.

"Said with truth and dignity," said Mr. Dad. "You have put my opinion, Sir Eliphaz, better than I could have put it myself. I thank you."

He coughed briefly.

§ 7

"The question you put to me I have put to myself," said Mr. Huss, and thought deeply for a little while....

"No, I do not feel convicted of wrong-doing. I still believe the work I set myself to do was right, right in spirit and intention, right in plan and method. You invite me to confess my faith broken and in the dust; and my faith was never so sure. There is a God in my heart, in my heart at least there is a God, who has always guided me to right and who guides me now. My conscience remains unassailable. These afflictions that you speak of as trials and warnings I can only see as inexplicable disasters. They perplex me, but they do not cow me. They strike me as pointless and irrelevant events."

"But this is terrible!" said Mr. Dad, deeply shocked.

"You push me back, Sir Eliphaz, from the discussion of our school affairs to more fundamental questions. You have raised the problem of the moral government of the world, a problem that has been distressing my mind since I first came here to Sundering, whether indeed failure is condemnation and success the sunshine of God's approval. You believe that the great God of the stars and seas and mountains is attentive to our conduct and responds to it. His sense of right is the same sense of right as ours; he endorses a common aim. Your prosperity is the mark of your harmony with that supreme God...."

"I wouldn't go so far as that," Mr. Dad interjected. "No. No arrogance."

"And my misfortunes express his disapproval. Well, I have believed that; I have believed that the rightness of a schoolmaster's conscience must needs be the same thing as the rightness of destiny, I too had fallen into that comforting persuasion of prosperity; but this series of smashing experiences I have had, culminating in your proposal to wipe out the whole effect and significance of my life, brings me face to face with the fundamental question whether the order of the great universe, the God of the stars, has any regard or relationship whatever to the problems of our consciences and the efforts of man to do right. That is a question that echoes to me down the ages. So far I have always professed myself a Christian...."

"Well, I should hope so," said Mr. Dad, "considering the terms of the school's foundation."

"For, I take it, the creeds declare in a beautiful symbol that the God who is present in our hearts is one with the universal father and at the same time his beloved Son, continually and eternally begotten from the universal fatherhood, and crucified only to conquer. He has come into our poor lives to raise them up at last to Himself. But to believe that is to believe in the significance and continuity of the whole effort of mankind. The life of man must be like the perpetual spreading of a fire. If right and wrong are to perish together indifferently, if there is aimless and fruitless suffering, if there opens no hope for an eternal survival in consequences of all good things, then there is no meaning in such a belief as Christianity. It is a mere superstition of priests and sacrifices, and I have read things into it that were never truly there. The rushlight of our faith burns in a windy darkness that will see no dawn."

"Nay," said Sir Eliphaz, "nay. If there is God in your work we cannot destroy it."

"You are doing your best," said Mr. Huss, "and now I am not sure that you will fail.... At one time I should have defied you, but now I am not sure.... I have sat here through some dreary and dreadful days, and lain awake through some interminable nights; I have thought of many things that men in their days of prosperity are apt to dismiss from their minds; and I am no longer sure of the goodness of the world without us or in the plan of Fate. Perhaps it is only in us within our hearts that the light of God flickers— and flickers insecurely. Where we had thought a God, somehow akin to ourselves, ruled in the universe, it may be there is nothing but black emptiness and a coldness worse than cruelty."

Mr. Dad was about to interrupt, and restrained himself by a

great effort.

"It is a commonplace of pietistic works that natural things are perfect things, and that the whole world of life, if it were not for the sinfulness of man, would be perfect. Paley, you will remember, Sir Eliphaz, in his 'Evidences of Christianity,' from which we have both suffered, declares that this earth is manifestly made for the happiness of the sentient beings living thereon. But I ask you to consider for a little and dispassionately, whether life through all its stages, up to and including man, is not rather a scheme of uneasiness, imperfect satisfaction, and positive miseries...."

§ 8

"Aren't we getting a bit out of our depth in all this?" Mr. Dad burst out. "Put it at that—out of our depth.... What does this sort of carping and questioning amount to, Mr. Huss? Does it do us any good? Does it help us in the slightest degree? Why should we go into all this? Why can't we be humble and leave these deep questions to those who make a specialty of dealing with them? We don't know the ropes. We can't. Here are you and Mr. Farr, for instance, both of you whole-time schoolmasters so to speak; here's Sir Eliphaz toiling night and day to make simple cheap suitable homes for the masses, who probably won't say thank you to him when they see them; here's me an overworked engineer and understaffed most cruelly, not to speak of the most unfair and impossible labour demands, so that you never know where you are and what they won't ask you next. And in the midst of it all we are to start an argey-bargey about the goodness of God!

"We're busy men, Mr. Huss. What do we know of the world being a scheme of imperfect satisfaction and what all? Where does it come in I What's its practical value? Words it is, all words, and getting away from the plain and definite question we came to talk over and settle and have done with. Such talk, I will confess, makes me uncomfortable. Give me the Bible and the simple religion I learnt at my mother's knee. That's good enough for me. Can't we just have faith and leave all these questions alone? What are men in reality? After all their arguments. Worms. Just worms. Well then, let's have the decency to behave as such and stick to business, and do our best in that state of life unto which it has pleased God to call us. That's what 7 say," said Mr. Dad.

He jerked his head back, coughed shortly, adjusted his tie, and nodded to Mr. Farr in a resolute manner.

"A simple, straightforward, commercial and technical education," he added by way of an explanatory colophon. "That's what we're after."

§ 9

Mr. Huss stared absently at Mr. Dad for some moments, and then resumed:

"Let us look squarely at this world about us. What is the true lot of life? Is there the slightest justification for assuming that our conceptions of right and happiness are reflected anywhere in the outward universe? Is there, for instance, much animal happiness! Do health and well-being constitute the normal state of animals?"

He paused. Mr. Dad got up, and stood looking out of the window with his back to Mr. Huss. "Pulling nature to pieces," he said over his shoulder. He turned and urged further, with a snarl of bitterness in his voice: " Suppose things are so, what is the good of our calling attention to it? Where's the benefit?" But the attitude of Sir Eliphaz conveyed a readiness to listen.

"Before I became too ill to go out here," said Mr. Huss, " I went for a walk in the country behind this place. I was weary before I started, but I was impelled to go by that almost irresistible desire that will seize upon one at times to get out of one's immediate surroundings. I wanted to escape from this wretched room, and I wanted to be alone, secure from interruptions, and free to think in peace. There was a treacherous promise in the day outside, much sunshine and a breeze. I had heard of woods a mile or so inland, and that conjured up a vision of cool green shade and kindly streams beneath the trees and of the fellowship of shy and gentle creatures. So I went out into the heat and into the dried and salted east wind, through glare and inky shadows, across many more fields than I had expected, until I came to some woods and then to a neglected park, and there for a time I sat down to rest....

"But I could get no rest. The turf was unclean through the presence of many sheep, and in it there was a number of close-growing but very sharply barbed thistles; and after a little time I realized that harvesters, those minute red beasts that creep upon one in the chalk lands and burrow into the skin and produce an almost intolerable itching, abounded. I got up again and went on, hoping in vain to find some fence or gate on which I might rest more comfortably. There were many flies and gnats, many more than there are here and of different sorts, and they persecuted me more and more. They surrounded me in a humming cloud, and I had to wave my walking-stick about my head all the time to keep them off me. I felt too exhausted to walk back, but there was, I knew, a village a mile or so ahead where I hoped to find some conveyance in which I might return by road....

"And as I struggled along in this fashion I came upon first one thing and then another, so apt to my mood that they might have been put there by some adversary. First it was a very young rabbit indeed, it was scarcely as long as my hand, which some cruel thing had dragged from its burrow. The back of its head had been bitten open and was torn and bloody, and the flies rose from its oozing wounds to my face like a cloud of witnesses. Then as I went on, trying to distract my mind from the memory of this pitiful dead thing by looking about me for something more agreeable, I discovered a row of little brown objects in a hawthorn bush, and going closer found they were some half-dozen victims of a butcherbird— beetles, fledgelings, and a mouse or so— spiked on the thorns. They were all twisted into painful attitudes, as if each had suffered horribly and challenged me by the last gesture of its limbs to judge between it and its creator.... And a little further on a gaunt, villainous-looking cat with rusty black fur that had bare patches suddenly ran upon me out of a side path; it had something in its mouth which it abandoned at the sight of me and left writhing at my feet, a pretty crested bird, very mangled, that flapped in flat circles upon the turf, unable to rise. A fit of weak and reasonless rage came upon me at this, and seeing the cat halt some yards away and turn to regard me and move as

63

if to recover its victim, I rushed at it and pursued it, shouting. Then it occurred to me that it would be kinder if, instead of a futile pursuit of the wretched cat, I went back and put an end to the bird's sufferings. For a time I could not find it, and I searched for it in the bushes in a fever to get it killed, groaning and cursing as I did so. When I found it, it fought at me with its poor bleeding wings and snapped its beak at me, and made me feel less like a deliverer than a murderer. I hit it with my stick, and as it still moved I stamped it to death with my feet. I fled from its body in an agony. 'And this,' I cried, 'this hell revealed, is God's creation!'"

"Tcha," exclaimed Mr. Dad.

"Suddenly it seemed to me that scales had fallen from my eyes and that I saw the whole world plain. It was as if the universe had put aside a mask it had hitherto worn, and shown me its face, and it was a face of boundless evil.... It was as if a power of darkness sat over me and watched me with a mocking gaze, and for the rest of that day I could think of nothing but the feeble miseries of living things. I was tortured, and all life was tortured with me. I failed to find the village I sought; I strayed far, I got back here at last long after dark, stopping sometimes by the wayside to be sick, sometimes kneeling or lying down for a time to rest, shivering and burning with an increasing fever.

"I had, as you know, been the first to find poor Williamson lying helpless among the acids; that ghastly figure and the burnt bodies of the two boys who died in School House haunt my mind constantly; but what was most in my thoughts on that day when the world of nature showed its teeth to me was the wretchedness of animal life. I do not know why that should have seemed more pitiful to me, and more fundamental, but it did. Human suffering, perhaps, is complicated by moral issues; man can look before and after and find remote justifications and stern consolations outside his present experiences; but the poor birds and beasts, they have only their present experiences and their individual lives cut off and shut in. How can there be righteousness in any scheme that afflicts them? I thought of one creature after another, and I could imagine none that had more than an occasional gleam of false and futile satisfaction between suffering and suffering. And today, gentlemen, as I sit here with you, the same dark stream of conviction pours through my mind.. I feel that life is a weak and inconsequent stirring amidst the dust of space and time, incapable of overcoming even its internal dissensions, doomed to phases of delusion, to irrational and undeserved punishments, to vain complainings and at last to extinction.

"Is there so much as one healthy living being in the world? I question it. As I wandered that day, I noted the trees as I had never noted them before. There was not one that did not show a stricken or rotten branch, or that was not studded with the stumps of lost branches decaying backwards towards the main stem; from every fork came dark stains of corruption, the bark was twisted and contorted and fungoid protrusions proclaimed the hidden mycelium of disease. The leaves were spotted with warts and blemishes, and gnawed and bitten by a myriad enemies. I noted too that the turf under my feet was worn and scorched and weary; gossamer threads and spiders of a hundred sorts trapped the multitudinous insects in the wilted autumnal undergrowth; the hedges were a slow conflict of thrusting and strangulating plants in which every individual was more or less crippled or stunted. Most of these plants were armed like assassins; they had great thorns or stinging hairs; some ripened poisonous berries. And this was the reality of life; this was no exceptional mood of things, but a revelation of things established. I had been blind and now I saw. Even as these woods and thickets were, so was all the world....

"I had been reading in a book I had chanced to pick up in this lodging, about the jungles of India, which many people think of as a vast wealth of splendid and luxuriant vegetation. For the greater part of the year they are hot and thorny wastes of brown, dead and mouldering matter. Comes the steaming downpour of the rains; and then for a little while there is a tangled rush of fighting greenery, jostling, choking, torn and devoured by a multitude of beasts and by a horrible variety of insects that the hot moisture has called to activity. Then under the dry breath of the destroyer the exuberance stales and withers, everything ripens and falls, and the jungle relapses again into sullen heat and gloomy fermentation. And in truth everywhere the growth season is a wild scramble into existence, the rest of the year a complicated massacre. Even in our British climate is it not plain to you how the summer outlasts the lavish promise of the spring? In our spring there is no doubt an air of hope, of budding and blossoming; there is the nesting and singing of birds, a certain cleanness of the air, an emergence of primary and comparatively innocent things; but hard upon that freshness follow the pests and parasites, the creatures that corrupt and sting, the minions of waste and pain and lassitude and fever....

"You may say that I am dwelling too much upon the defects in the lives of plants which do not feel, and of insects and small creatures which may feel in a different manner from ourselves;

but indeed their decay and imperfection make up the common texture of life. Even the things that live are only half alive. You may argue that at least the rarer, larger beasts bring with them a certain delight and dignity into the world. But consider the lives of the herbivora; they are all hunted creatures; fear is their habit of mind; even the great Indian buffalo is given to panic flights. They are incessantly worried by swarms of insects. When they are not apathetic they appear to be angry, exasperated with life; their seasonal outbreaks of sex are evidently a violent torment to them, an occasion for fierce bellowings, mutual persecution and desperate combats. Such beasts as the rhinoceros or the buffalo are habitually in a rage; they will run amuck for no conceivable reason, and so too will many elephants, betraying a sort of organic spite against all other living things....

"And if we turn to the great carnivores, who should surely be the lords of the jungle world, their lot seems to be not one whit more happy. The tiger leads a life of fear; a dirty scrap of rag will turn him from his path. Much of his waking life is prowling hunger; when he kills he eats ravenously, he eats to the pitch of discomfort; he lies up afterwards in reeds or bushes, savage, disinclined to move. The hunter must beat him out, and he comes out sluggishly and reluctantly to die. His paws, too, are strangely tender; a few miles of rock will make them bleed, they gather thorns.... His mouth is so foul that his bite is a poisoned bite....

"All that day I struggled against this persuasion that the utmost happiness of any animal is at best like a transitory smile on a grim and inhuman countenance. I tried to recall some humorous and contented-looking creatures....

"That only recalled a fresh horror....

"You will have seen pictures and photographs of penguins. They will have conveyed to you the sort of effect I tried to recover. They express a quaint and jolly gravity, an aldermanic contentment. But to me now the mere thought of a penguin raises a vision of distress. I will tell you.... One of my old boys came to me a year or so ago on his return from a South Polar expedition; he told me the true story of these birds. Their lives, he said—he was speaking more particularly of the king penguin— are tormented by a monstrously exaggerated maternal instinct, an instinct shared by both sexes, which is a necessary condition of survival in the crowded rookeries of that frozen environment. And that instinct makes life one long torment for them. There is always a great smashing of eggs there through various causes; there is an excessive mortality among the chicks; they slip down crevasses, they freeze to death and so forth, three-quarters of each year's brood perish, and without this extravagant passion the species would become extinct. So that every bird is afflicted with a desire and anxiety to brood upon and protect a chick. But each couple produces no more than one egg a year; eggs get broken, they roll away into the water, there is always a shortage, and every penguin that has an egg has to guard it jealously, and each one that has not an egg is impelled to steal or capture one. Some in their distress will mother pebbles or scraps of ice, some fortunate in possession will sit for days without leaving the nest in spite of the gnawings of the intense Antarctic hunger. To leave a nest for a moment is to tempt a robber, and the intensity of the emotions aroused is shown by the fact that they will fight to the death over a stolen egg. You see that these pictures of rookeries of apparently comical birds are really pictures of poor dim-minded creatures

68

worried and strained to the very limit, of their powers. That is what their lives have always been....

"But the king penguin draws near the end of its history. Let me tell you how its history is closing. Let me tell you of what is happening in the peaceful Southern Seas— now. This old boy of mine was in great distress because of a vile traffic that has arisen.... Unless it is stopped, it will destroy these rookeries altogether. These birds are being murdered wholesale for their oil. Parties of men land and club them upon their nests, from which the poor, silly things refuse to stir. The dead and stunned, the living and the dead together, are dragged away and thrust into iron crates to be boiled down for their oil. The broken living with the dead.... Each bird yields about a farthing's profit, but it pays to kill them at that, and so the thing is done. The people who run these operations, you see, have had a sound commercial training. They believe that when God gives us power He means us to use it, and that what is profitable is just."

"Well, really," protested Mr. Dad. "Really!"

Mr. Farr also betrayed a disposition to speak. He cleared his throat, his uneasy hands worried the edge of the table, his face shone. "Sir Eliphaz," he said....

"Let me finish," said Mr. Huss, " for I have still to remind you of the most stubborn facts of all in such an argument as this. Have you ever thought of the significance of such creatures as the entozoa, and the vast multitudes of other sorts of specialized parasites whose very existence is cruelty? There are thousands of orders and genera of insects, Crustacea, arachnids, worms, and lowlier things, which are adapted in the most complicated way to prey upon the living and suffering tissues of their fellow creatures, and which can live in no other way. Have you ever thought what that means! If forethought framed these horrors what sort of benevolence was there in that forethought? I will not distress you by describing the life cycles of any of these creatures too exactly. You must know of many of them. I will not dwell upon those wasps, for example, which lay their eggs in the living bodies of victims which the young will gnaw to death slowly day by day as they develop, nor will I discuss this unmeaning growth of cells which has made my body its soil.... Nor any one of our thousand infectious fevers that fall upon us— without reason, without justice....

"Man is of all creatures the least subjected to internal parasites. In the brief space of a few hundred thousand years he has changed his food, his habitat and every attitude and habit of his life, and comparatively few species, thirty or forty at most, I am told, have been able to follow his changes and specialize themselves to him under these fresh conditions; yet even man can entertain some fearful guests. Every time you drink open water near a sheep pasture you may drink the larval liver fluke, which will make your liver a little township of vile creatures until they eat it up, until they swarm from its oozing ruins into your body cavity and destroy you. In Europe this is a rare fate for a man, but in China there are wide regions where the fluke abounds and rots the life out of thousands of people.... The fluke is but one sample of such feats of the Creator. An unwashed leaf of lettuce may be the means of planting a parasitic cyst in your brain to dethrone your reason; a feast of underdone pork may transfer to you from the swine the creeping death torture of trichinosis.... But all that men suffer in these matters is nothing to the suffering of the beasts. The torments of the beasts are finished and complete. My biological master tells me that he rarely opens a cod or dogfish without finding bunches of some sort of worm or such like pallid lodger in possession. He has rows of little tubes with the things he has found in the bodies of rabbits....

"But I will not disgust you further....

"Is this a world made for the happiness of sentient things?

"I ask you? how is it possible for man to be other than a rebel in the face of such facts'? How can he trust the Maker who has designed and elaborated and finished these parasites in their endless multitude and variety? For these things are not in the nature of sudden creations and special judgments; they have been produced fearfully and wonderfully by a process of evolution as slow and deliberate as our own. How can Man trust such a Maker to treat him fairly? Why should we shut our eyes to things that stare us in the face? Either the world of life is the creation of a being inspired by a malignancy at once filthy, petty and enormous, or it displays a carelessness, an indifference, a disregard for justice.... "

The voice of Mr. Huss faded out.

§ 10

For some time Mr. Farr had been manifesting signs of impatience. The pause gave him his opportunity. He spoke with a sort of restrained volubility.

"Sir Eliphaz, Mr. Dad, after what has passed in relation to myself, I would have preferred to have said nothing in this discussion. Nothing. So far as I myself am concerned, I will still say nothing. But upon some issues it is impossible to keep silence. Mr. Huss has said some terrible things, things that must surely never be said at Woldingstanton....

"Think of what such teaching as this may mean among young and susceptible boys! Think of such stuff in the school pulpit! Chary as I am of all wrangling, and I would not set myself up for a moment to wrangle against Mr. Huss, yet I feel that this cavilling against God's universe, this multitude of evil words, must be answered. It is imperative to answer it, plainly and sternly. It is our duty to God, who has made us what we are....

"Mr. Huss, in your present diseased state you seem incapable of realizing the enormous egotism of all this depreciation of God's marvels. But indeed you have suffered from that sort of incapacity always. It is no new thing. Have I not chafed under your arrogant assurance for twelve long years? Your right, now as ever, is the only right; your doctrine alone is pure. Would that God could speak and open his lips against you! How his voice would shatter you and us and everything about us! How you would shrivel amidst your blasphemies!

"Excuse me, gentlemen, if I am too forcible," said Mr. Farr, moistening his white lips, but Mr. Dad nodded fierce approval.

Thus encouraged, Mr. Farr proceeded. "When first I came into this room, Mr. Huss, I was full of pity for your affliction— I think we all were— we were pitiful; but now it is clear to me that God exacts from you less than your iniquity deserves. Surely the supreme sin is pride. You criticize and belittle God's universe, but what sort of a universe would you give us, Mr. Huss, if you were the Creator? Pardon me if I startle you, gentlemen, but that is a fair question to ask. For it is clear to me now, Mr. Huss, that no less than that will satisfy you. Woldingstanton, for all the wonders you have wrought there, in spite of the fact that never before and never again can there be such a head, in spite of the fact that you have lit such a candle there as may one day set the world ablaze, is clearly too small a field for you. Headmaster of the universe is your position. Then, and then alone, could you display your gifts to the full. Then cats would cease to eat birds, and trees grow on in perfect symmetry until they cumbered the sky. I can dimly imagine the sort of world that it would be; the very fleas reformed and trained under your hand, would be flushed with health and happiness and doing the work of boy scouts; every blade of grass would be at least six feet long. As for the liver fluke— but I cannot solve the problem of the liver fluke. I suppose you will provide euthanasia for all the parasites...."

Abruptly Mr. Farr passed from this vein of terrible humour to an earnest and pleading manner. "Mr. Huss, with mortal danger so close to you, I entreat you to reconsider all this wild and wicked talk of yours. You take a few superficial aspects of the world and frame a judgment on them; you try with the poor foot-rule of your mind to measure the plans of God, plans which are longer than the earth, wider than the sea. I ask you, how can such insolence help yon in this supreme emergency? There can be little time left...."

Providence was manifestly resolved to give Mr. Farr the maximum of dramatic effect. "But what is this?" said Mr. Farr. He stood up and looked out of the window.

Somebody had rung the bell, and now, with an effect of impatience, was rapping at the knocker of Sea View.

73

IV. — DO WE TRULY DIE?

§ 1

MRS. CROOME was heard in the passage, someone was admitted, there were voices, and the handle of the parlour door was turned. "'Asn't E come, then?" they heard the voice of Mrs. Croome through the opening. Dr. Elihu Barrack appeared in the doorway.

He was a round-headed young man with a clean-shaven face, a mouth that was determinedly determined and slightly oblique, a short nose, and a general expression of resolution; the fact that he had an artificial leg was scarcely perceptible in his bearing. He considered the four men before him for a moment, and then addressed himself to Mr. Huss in a tone of brisk authority. "You ought to be in bed," he said.

"I had this rather important discussion," said Mr. Huss, with a gesture portending introductions.

"But sitting up will fatigue you," the doctor insisted, sticking to his patient.

"It won't distress me so much as leaving these things unsaid would have done."

"Opinions may differ upon that," said Mr. Farr darkly.

"We are still far from any settlement of our difficulties," said Sir Eliphaz to the universe.

"I have indicated my view at any rate," said Mr. Huss. "I

74

suppose now Sir Alpheus is here—"

"He isn't here," said Dr. Barrack neatly. "He telegraphs to say that he is held up, and will come by the next train. So you get a reprieve, Mr. Huss."

"In that case I shall go on talking."

"You had better go to bed."

"No. I couldn't lie quiet." And Mr. Huss proceeded to name his guests to Dr. Barrack, who nodded shortly to each of them in turn, and said: "Pleased-t-meet you." His face betrayed no excess of pleasure. His eye was hard. He remained standing, as if waiting for them to display symptoms.

"Our discussion has wandered far," said Sir Eliphaz. "Our original business here was to determine the future development of Woldingstanton School, which we think should be made more practical and technical than hitherto, and less concerned with history and philosophy than it has been under Mr. Huss. (Won't you sit down, Doctor?) "

The doctor sat down, still watching Sir Eliphaz with hard intelligence.

"Well, we have drifted from that," Sir Eliphaz continued.

"Not so far as you may think," said Mr. Huss.

"At any rate Mr. Huss has been regaling us with a discourse upon the miseries of life, how we are all eaten up by parasites and utterly wretched, and how everything is wretched and this an accursed world ruled either by a cruel God or a God so careless as to be practically no God at all."

"Nice stuff for nineteen eighteen *A.D.*," said Mr. Dad, putting much meaning into the "A.D."

"Since I left Woldingstanton and came here," said Mr. Huss, "I have done little else but think. I have not slept during the night, I have had nothing to occupy me during the day, and I have been thinking about fundamental things. I have been forced to revise my faith, and to look more closely than I have ever done before into the meaning of my beliefs and into my springs of action. I have been wrenched away from that habitual confidence in the order of things which seemed the more natural state for a mind to be in. But that has only widened a difference that already existed between me and these three gentlemen, and that was showing very plainly in the days when success still justified my grip upon Woldingstanton. Suddenly, swiftly, I have had misfortune following upon misfortune— without cause or justification. I am thrown now into the darkest doubt and dismay; the universe seems harsh and black to me; whereas formerly I believed that at the core of it and universally pervading it was the Will of a God of Light.... I have always denied, even when my faith was undimmed, that the God of Righteousness ruled this world in detail and entirely, giving us day by day our daily rewards and punishments. These gentlemen on the contrary do believe that. They say that God does rule the world traceably and directly, and that success is the measure of his approval and pain and suffering the fulfilment of unrighteousness. And as for what has this lo do with education—it has all to do with education. You can settle no practical questions until you have settled such disputes as this. Before you can prepare boys to play their part in the world you must ask what is this world for which you prepare them; is it a tragedy or comedy? What is the nature of this drama in which they are to play?"

Dr. Barrack indicated that this statement was noted and approved.

"For clearly," said Mr. Huss, " if success is the justification of life you must train for success. There is no need for men to understand life, then, so long as they do their job in it. That is the opinion of these governors of mine. It has been the opinion of most men of the world— always. Obey the Thing that Is! that is the lesson they would have taught to my boys. Acquiesce. Life for them is not an adventure, not a struggle, but simply obedience and the enjoyment of rewards.... That, Dr. Barrack, is what such a technical education as they want set up at Woldingstanton really means....

"But I have believed always and taught always that what God demands from man is his utmost effort to co-operate and understand. I have taught the imagination, first and most; I have made knowledge, knowledge of what man is and what man's world is and what man may be, which is the adventure of mankind, the substance of all my teaching. At Woldingstanton I have taught philosophy; I have taught the whole history of mankind. If I could not have done that without leaving chemistry and physics, mathematics and languages out of the curriculum altogether I would have left them out. And you see why, Dr. Barrack."

"I see your position certainly," said Dr. Barrack.

"And now that my heavens are darkened, now that my eyes have been opened to the wretchedness, futility and horror in the texture of life, I still cling, I cling more than ever, to the spirit of righteousness within me. If there is no God, no mercy, no human kindliness in the great frame of space and time, if life is a writhing torment, an itch upon one little planet, and the stars away there in the void no more than huge empty flares, signifying nothing, then all the brighter shines the flame of God in my heart. If the God in my heart is no son of any heavenly father then is he Prometheus the rebel; it does not shake my faith that he is the Master for whom I will live and die. And all the more do I cling to this fire of human tradition we have lit upon this little planet, if it is the one gleam of spirit in all the windy vastness of a dead and empty universe."

Dr. Barrack seemed about to interrupt with some comment, and then, it was manifest, deferred his interpolation.

"Loneliness and littleness," said Mr. Huss, "harshness in the skies above and in the texture of all things. If so it is that things are, so we must see them. Every baby in its mother's arms feels safe in a safe creation; every child in its home. Many men and women have lived ^and died happy in that illusion of security. But this war has torn away the veil of illusion from millions of men.... Mankind is coming of age. We can see life at last for what it is and what it is not. Here we spin upon a ball of rock and nickel- steel, upon which a film of water, a few score miles of air, lie like the bloom upon a plum. All about that ball is space unfathomable; all the suns and stars are mere grains of matter scattered through a vastness that is otherwise utterly void. To that thin bloom upon a particle we are confined; if we tunnel down into the earth, presently it is too hot for us to live; if we soar five miles into the air we freeze, the blood runs out of our vessels into our lungs, we die suffocated and choked with blood....

"Out of the litter of muds and gravels that make the soil of the world we have picked some traces of the past of our race and the past of life. In our observatories and laboratories we have gleaned some hints of its future. We have a vision of the opening of the story, but the first pages we cannot read. "We discover life, a mere stir amidst the mud, creeping along the littoral of warm and shallow seas in the brief nights and days of a swiftly rotating earth. We follow through vast ages the story of life's extension into the waters, and its invasion of the air and land. Plants creep upon the land and raise themselves by stems towards the sun; a few worms and crustaceans follow, insects appear; and at length come our amphibious ancestors, breathing air by means of a swimming bladder used as a lung. From the first the land animals are patched-up creatures. They eke out the fish ear they inherit by means of an ear drum made out of a gill slit. You can trace scale and fin in bone and limb. At last this green scum of vegetable life with the beasts entangled in its meshes creeps in the form of forests over the hills; grass spreads across the plains, and great animals follow it out into the open. What does it all signify? No more than green moss spreading over an old tile. Steadily the earth cools and the day lengthens. Through long ages of warmth and moisture the wealth of unmeaning life increases; come ages of chill and retrocession, glacial periods, and periods when whole genera and orders die out. Comes man at last, the destroyer, the war-maker, setting fire to the world, burning the forests, exhausting the earth. What hope has he in the end? Always the day drags longer and longer and always the sun radiates its energy away. A time will come when the sun will glow dull red in the heavens, shorn of all its beams, and neither rising nor setting. A day will come when the earth will be as dead and frozen as the moon.... A spirit in our hearts, the God of mankind, cries 'No!' but is there any voice outside us in all the cold and empty universe that echoes that 'No'?"

§ 2

"Ah, Mr. Huss, Mr. Huss!" said Sir Eliphaz.

His eye seemed seeking some point of attachment, and found it at last in the steel engraving of Queen Victoria giving a Bible to a dusky potentate, which adorned the little parlour.

"Your sickness colours your vision," said Sir Eliphaz. "What you say is so profoundly true and so utterly false. Mysteriously evolved, living as you say in a mere bloom of air and moisture upon this tiny planet, how could we exist, how could we continue, were we not sustained in every moment by the Mercy and Wisdom of God? The flimsier life is, the greater the wonder of his Providence. Not a sparrow," said Sir Eliphaz, and then enlarging the metaphor with a boom in his voice, "not a hair of my head, falls to the ground without His knowledge and consent.... I am a man much occupied. I cannot do the reading I would. But while you have been reviling the works of God I have been thinking of some wonders.

Sir Eliphaz lifted up a hand with thumb and finger opposed, as though he held some exquisite thing therein.

"The human eye," said Sir Eliphaz, with an intensity of appreciation that brought tears to his own....

"The cross fertilization of plants....

"The marvellous transformations of the higher insects....

"The highly elaborate wing scales of the Lepidoptera.

"The mercy that tempers the wind to the shorn lamb....

"The dark warm marvels of embryology; the order and rhythm and obedience with which the cells of the fertilized ovum divide to build up the perfect body of a living thing, yea, even of a human being— in God's image. First there is one cell, then two; the process of division is extremely beautiful and is called, I believe, *karyokinesis*; then after the two come four, each knows his part, each divides certainly and marvellously; eight, sixteen, thirty-two.... Each of those thirty-two cells is a complete thirty-second part of a man. Presently this cell says, 'I become a hair'; this, 'a blood corpuscle,' this 'a cell in the brain of a man, to mirror the universe.' Each goes to his own appointed place....

"Would that we could do the like"! said Sir Eliphaz.

"Then consider water," said Sir Eliphaz. "I am not deeply versed in physical science, but there are certain things about water that fill me with wonder and amaze. All other liquids contract when they solidify. With one or two exceptions— useful in the arts. Water expands. Now water is a non- conductor of heat, and if water contracted and became heavier when it became ice, it would sink to the bottom of the polar seas and remain there unmelted. More ice would sink down to it, until all the ocean was ice and life ceased. But water does not do so. No!... Were it not for the vapour of water, which catches and entangles the sun's heat, this world would scorch by day and freeze by night. Mercy upon mercy, I myself," said Sir Eliphaz in tones of happy confession, " am ninety per cent, water.... We all are....

"And think how mercifully winter is tempered to us by the snow! When water freezes in the air in winter-time, it does not come pelting down as lumps of ice. Conceivably it might, and then where should we be? But it belongs to the hexagonal system— a system prone to graceful frameworks. It crystallizes into the most delicate and beautiful lace of six-rayed crystals— wonderful under the microscope. They flake delicately. They lie loosely one upon another. Out of ice is woven a warm garment like wool, white like wool because like wool it is full of air— a warm garment for bud and shoot....

"Then again— you revile God for the parasites he sends. But are they not sent to teach us a great moral lesson? Each one for himself and God for us all. Not so the parasites. They choose a life of base dependence. With that comes physical degeneration, swift and sure. They are the Socialists of nature. They lose their limbs. They lose colour, become blenched, unappetising beings, vile creatures of sloth—often microscopic. Do they not urge us by their shameful lives to self help and exertion? Yet even parasites have a use! I am told that were it not for parasitic bacteria man could not digest his food. A lichen again is made up of an alga and a fungus, mutually parasitic. That is called symbiosis— living together for a mutual benefit. Maybe every one of those thousands of parasites you deem so horrible is working its way upward towards an arrangement—"

Sir Eliphaz weighed his words: "Some mutually advantageous arrangement with its host. A paying guest.

"And finally," said Sir Eliphaz, with the roll of distant thunder in his voice, " think of the stately procession of life upon the earth, through a myriad of forms the glorious crescendo of evolution, up to its climax, man. What a work is man! The paragon of creation, the microcosm of the cosmos, the ultimate birth of time.... And you would have us doubt the guiding hand!"

He ceased with a gesture.

Mr. Dad made a noise like responses in church.

§ 3

"A certain beauty in the world is no mark of God's favour," said Mr. Huss. "There is no beauty one may not balance by an equal ugliness. The wart-hog and the hyaena, the tapeworm and the stinkhorn, are equally God's creations. Nothing you have said points to anything but a cold indifference towards us of this order in which we live. Beauty happens; it is not given. Pain, suffering, happiness; there is no heed. Only in the heart of man burns the fire of righteousness."

For a time Mr. Huss was silent. Then he went on answering Sir Eliphaz.

"You spoke of the wonder of the cross-fertilization of plants. But do you not know that half these curious and elaborate adaptations no longer work? Scarcely was their evolution completed before the special need that produced them ceased. Half the intricate flowers you see are as futile as the ruins of Palmyra. They are self-fertilized or wind-fertilized. The transformation of the higher insects which give us our gnats and wasps, our malaria and apple- maggots in due season, are a matter for human astonishment rather than human gratitude. If there is any design in these strange and intricate happenings, surely it is the design of a misplaced and inhuman ingenuity. The scales of the lepidoptera, again, have wasted their glittering splendours for millions of years. If they were meant for man, why do the most beautiful species fly by night in the tropical forests? As for the human eye, oculists and opticians are scarcely of your opinion. You hymn the peculiar properties of water that make life possible. They make it possible. Do they make it other than it is?

"You have talked of the marvels of embryonic growth in the egg. I admit the wonderful precision of the process; but how does it touch my doubts? Either it confuses them, as though the God who rules the world ruled not so much in love as in irony. Wonderfully indeed do the cells divide and the chromoplasts of the division slide along their spindle lines. They divide not as if a divine hand guided them but with remorseless logic, with the pitiless consistency of a mathematical process. They divide and marshal themselves and turn this way and that, to make an idiot, to make a congenital cripple. Millions of such miracles pile up— and produce the swaying drunkard at the pot-house door.

"You talk of the crescendo of evolution, of the first beginnings of life, and how the scheme unfolds until it culminates in us— *us*, here, under these circumstances, you and Mr. Dad and Farr and me— waiting for the knife. Would that I could see any such crescendo! I see change indeed and change and change, without plan and without heart. Consider for example the migrations of birds across the Mediterranean, and the tragic absurdity of its incidents. Ages ago, and for long ages, there stretched continuous land connexions from Africa to Europe. Then the instinct was formed; the birds flew over land from the heated south to the northern summer to build and breed. Slowly age by age the seas crept over those necks of land. Those linking tracts have been broken now for a hundred thousand years, and yet over a constantly widening sea, in which myriads perish exhausted, instinct, blind and pitiless, still drives those birds. And again think of those vain urgencies for some purpose long since forgotten, that drive the swarming lemmings to their fate. And look at man, your evolution's crown; consider his want of balance, the invalidism of his women, the extravagant disproportion of his desires. Consider the Becord of the Bocks honestly and frankly, and where can you trace this crescendo you suggest? There have been great ages of marvellous treeferns and wonderful forest swamps, and all those glorious growths have died. They did not go on; they reached a climax and died; another sort of plant succeeded them. Then think of all that wonderful fauna of the Mesozoic times, the age of Leviathan; the theriodonts, reptilian beasts, the leaping dinosaurs, the mososaurs and suchlike monsters of the deep, the bat-winged pterodactyls, the plesiosaurs and ichthyosaurs. Think of the marvels of the Mesozoic seas; the thousands of various ammonites, the wealth of fish life. Across all that world of life swept death, as the wet fingers of a child wipe a drawing from a slate. They left no descendants, they clambered to a vast variety and complexity and ceased. The dawn of the Eocene was the bleak dawn of a denuded world. Crescendo if you will, but thereafter diminuendo, pianissimo. And then once again from fresh obscure starting-points far down the stem life swelled, and swelled again, only to dwindle. The world we live in to-day is a meagre spectacle beside the abundance of the earlier Tertiary time, when Behemoth in a thousand forms, Deinotherium, Titanotherium, Helladotherium, sabre-toothed tiger, a hundred sorts of elephant, and the like, pushed through the jungles that are now this mild world of to-day. Where is that crescendo now? Crescendo! Through those long ages our ancestors were hiding under leaves and climbing into trees to be out of the way of the crescendo. As the *motif* of a crescendo they sang exceedingly small. And now for a little while the world is ours, and we wax in our turn. To what good? To what end? Tell me, you who say the world is good, tell me the end. How can we escape at last the common fate under the darkling sky of a frozen world?"

He paused for some moments, weary with speaking.

"There is no comfort," he said, " in the flowers or the stars; no assurance in the past and no sure hope in the future. There is nothing but the God of faith and courage in the hearts of men.... And He gives no sign of power, no earnest of victory.... He gives no sign...."

Whereupon Sir Eliphaz breathed the word: *"Immortality!"*

"Let me say a word or two upon Immortality," said Sir Eliphaz, breaking suddenly into eagerness, " for that, I presume, is the thing we have forgotten. That, I see, is the difference between us and you, Mr. Huss; that is why we can sit here, content to play our partial roles, knowing full surely that some day the broken lines and inconsecutivenesses that perplex us in this life will all be revealed and resolved into their perfect circles, while you to whom this earthly life is all and final, you must needs be a rebel, you must needs preach a doctrine between defiance and despair.... If indeed death ended all! *Ah!* Then indeed you might claim that reason was on your side. The afflictions of man are very many. Why should I deny it?"

The patentee and chief proprietor of the Temanite blocks paused for a moment.

"Yes," he said, peering up through his eyebrows at the sky, " that is the real issue. Blind to that, you are blind to everything."

"I don't know whether I am with you on this question of immortality, Sir Eliphaz," warned Dr. Barrack, coughing shortly.

"For my part I'm altogether with him," said Mr. Dad. "If there is no immortal life—well, what's the good of being temperate and decent and careful for five and fifty years?"

Sir Eliphaz had decided now to drop all apologetics for the scheme of Nature.

"A place of trial, a place of stimulus and training," he said, "*Respice finem.* The clues are all— beyond."

"But if you really consider this world as a place for soul making," said Mr. Huss, " what do you think you are doing when you propose to turn Woldingstanton over to Farr?"

"At any rate," said Farr tartly, " we do not want soul-blackening and counsels of despair at Woldingstanton. We want the boys taught to serve and help first in this lowly economic sphere, cheerfully and enterprisingly, and then in higher things, before they pass on—"

"If death ends all, then what is the good of trying?" Mr. Dad said, still brooding over the question. "If I thought that—!"

He added with deep conviction, " I should let myself go.... Anyone would."

He blew heavily, stuck his hands in his pockets, and sat more deeply in his chair, an indignant man, a business man asked to give up something for nothing.

For a moment the little gathering hung, only too manifestly contemplating the spectacle of Mr. Dad amidst wine, women, and waistcoats without restraint, letting himself go, eating, drinking, and rejoicing, being a perfect devil, beeause on the morrow he had to die...

"Immortal," said Mr. Huss. "I did not expect immortality to come into this discussion.

"Are *you* immortal, Farr?" he asked abruptly.

"I hope so," said Mr. Farr. "Unworthy though I be."

"Exactly," said Mr. Huss. "And so that is the way out for us. You and I, Mr. Dad from his factory, and Sir Eliphaz from his building office, are to soar. It is all arranged for us, and that is why the tragic greatness of life is to be hidden from my boys....

"Yet even so," continued Mr. Huss, " I do not see why you should be so anxious for technical science and so hostile to the history of mankind."

"Because it is not a true history," said Sir Eliphaz, his hair waving about like the hair of a man electrified by fresh ideas. "Because it is a bunch of loose ends that are really not ends at all, but only beginnings that pass suddenly into the unseen. I admit that in this world nothing is rationalized, nothing is clearly just. I admit everything you say. But the reason? The reason? Because this life is only the first page of the great book we have to read. We sit here, Mr. Huss, like men in a waiting-room.... All this life is like waiting outside, in a place of some disorder, before being admitted to the wider reality, the larger sphere, where all the cruelties, all these confusions, everything—will be explained, justified— and set right."

He paused, and then perceiving that Mr. Huss was about to speak he resumed, raising his voice slightly.

"And I do not speak without my book in these matters," he said. "I have been greatly impressed— and, what is more, Lady Burrows has been greatly impressed, by the writings of two thoroughly scientific men, two thoroughly scientific men, Dr. Conan Doyle and Sir Oliver Lodge. Ever since she lost her younger sister early in life Lady Burrows has followed up this interest. It has been a great consolation to her. And the point is, as Sir Oliver insists in that wonderful book 'Raymond,' that continued existence in another world is as proven now as the atomic theory in chemistry. It is not a matter of faith, but knowledge. The partition is breached at last. We are in communication. News is coming through.... Scientific certainty...."

Sir Eliphaz cleared his throat. "We have already evidences and descriptions of the life into which we shall pass. Remember this is no idle talk, no deception by Sludges and the like; it is a great English scientific man who publishes these records; it is a great French philosopher, no less a man than that wonderful thinker— and *how* he thinks!— Professor Bergson, who counselled their publication. A glory of science and a glory of philosophy combine to reassure us. We walk at last upon a path of fact into that further world. We know already much. We know, for example, that those who have passed over to that higher plane have bodies still. That I found— comforting. Without that— one would feel *bleak*. But, the messages say, the internal organs are constituted differently. Naturally. As one would have expected. The dietary is, I gather, practically non-existent. Needless. As the outline is the same the space is, I presume, used for other purposes. Some sort of astral storage.... They do not bleed. An interesting fact. Lady Burrows' sister is now practically bloodless. And her teeth— she had lost several, she suffered greatly with her teeth her teeth— have all been replaced a beautiful set. Used now only for articulate speech."

"'Raymond' all over again," said the doctor.

"You have read the book!" said Sir Eliphaz.

The doctor grunted in a manner that mingled assent and disapproval. His expression betrayed the scientific bigot.

"We know now *details* of the passage," said Sir Eliphaz. "We have some particulars. We know, for instance, that people blown to pieces take some little time to reconstitute. There is a correlation between this corruptible body and the spirit body that replaces it. There is a sort of spirit doctor over there, very helpful in such cases. And burnt bodies, too, are a trouble.... The sexes are still distinct, but all the coarseness of sex is gone. The passions fade in that better world. Every passion. Even the habit of smoking and the craving for alcohol fade. Not at first. The newly dead will sometimes ask for a cigar. They are given cigars, higher-plane cigars, and they do not ask for more. There are no children born there. Nothing of that sort. That, it is very important to understand. *Here* is the place of birth; this is where lives begin. This coarse little planet is the seed-bed of life. When it has served its purpose and populated those higher planes, then indeed it may freeze, as you say. A mere empty hull. A seed-case that has served its purpose, mattering nothing. These are the thoughts, the comforting and beautiful thoughts, that receive the endorsement of our highest scientific and philosophical intelligences....One thinks of that life there, no doubt in some other dimension of space, that world arranged in *planes*— metaphorical planes, of course, in which people go to and fro, living in a sort of houses, surrounded by a sort of beautiful things, made, so we are told, from the smells of the things we have here. That is curious, but not irrational. Our favorite doggies will be there. Sublimated also. That thought has been a great comfort to Lady Burrows.... We had a dog called Fido, a leetle, teeny fellow— practically human....

"These blessed ones engage very largely in conversation. Other occupations I found difficult to trace. Raymond attended a sort of reception on the very highest plane. It was a special privilege. Perhaps a compliment to Sir Oliver. He met the truth of revealed religion, so to speak, personally. It was a wonderful moment. Sir Oliver suppresses the more solemn details. Lady Burrows intends to write to him. She is anxious for particulars. But I will not dilate, " said Sir Eliphaz. "I will not dilate."

"And you believe this *stuff*?" said the doctor in tones of the deepest disgust.

Sir Eliphaz waved himself upon the questioner.

"So far as poor earthly expressions can body forth spiritual things, " he hedged.

He regarded his colleagues with an eye of florid defiance. Both Mr. Farr and Mr. Dad had slightly shamefaced expressions, and Mr. Dad's ears were red.

Mr. Dad cleared his throat. "I'm sure there's something in it anyhow," said Mr. Dad hoarsely, doing his best in support.

"If I was born with a hare lip," said the doctor, "would *that* be put right? Do congenital idiots get sublimated? What becomes of a dog one has shot for hydrophobia?"

"To all of such questions," said Sir Eliphaz serenely, "the answer is we *don't* know. Why should we?"

§4

Mr. Huss seemed lost in meditation. His pale and sunken face and crumpled pose contrasted strongly with the bristling intellectual rectitude and mounting choler of Dr. Elihu Barrack.

"No, Sir Eliphaz," said Mr. Huss, and sighed.

"No," he repeated.

"What a poor phantom of a world these people conjure up! What a mockery of loss and love! The very mothers and lovers who mourn their dead will not believe their foolish stories. Restoration! It is a crowning indignity. It makes me think of nothing in the world but my dear boy's body, broken and crumpled, and some creature, half fool and half impostor, sitting upon it, getting between it and me, and talking cheap rubbish over it about planes of being and astral bodies....

"After all, you teach me, Sir Eliphaz, that life, for all its grossness and pain and horror, is not so bad as it might be— if such things as this were true. But it needs no sifting of the evidence to know they are untrue. No sane man believes this stuff for ten minutes together. It is impossible to believe it...."

Dr. Elihu Barrack applauded. Sir Eliphaz acted a fine self-restraint.

"They are contrary to the texture of everything we know," said Mr. Huss. "They are less convincing than the wildest dreams. By pain, by desire, by muscular effort, by the feeling of sunshine or of rain in the face, by their sense of justice and such-like essential things do men test the reality of appearances before them. This certainly is no reality. It has none of the *feel* of reality. I will not even argue about it. It is thrust now upon a suffering world as comfort, and even as comfort for people stunned and uncritical with grief it fails. You and Lady Burrows may be pleased to think that somehow you two, with your teeth restored and your complexions rejuvenated, will meet again the sublimation of your faithful Fido. At any rate, thank God for that, I know clearly that so I shall never meet my son. Never! He has gone from me...."

For some moments mental and physical suffering gripped him, and he could not speak; but his purpose to continue was so manifested by sweating face and gripping hand that no one spoke until he spoke again.

"Now let me speak plainly about Immortality. For surely I stand nearest to that possibility of all of us here. Immortality, then, is no such dodging away as you imagine, from this strange world which is so desolating, so dreadful, so inexplicable— and at times so utterly lonely. There may be a God in the universe or there may not be.... God, if he exists, can be terribly silent.... But if there is a God, he is a coherent God. If there is a God above and in the scheme of things, then not only you and I and my dead son, but the crushed frog and the trampled anthill *signify*. On that the God in my heart insists. There has to be an answer, not only to the death of my son but to the dying penguin roasted alive for a farthing's worth of oil. There must be an answer to the men who go in ships to do such things. There has to be a justification for all the filth and wretchedness of louse and fluke. I will not have you slipping by on the other side, chattering of planes of living and sublimated atoms, while there is a drunken mother or a man dying of cholera in this world. I will not hear of a God who is just a means for getting away. Whatever foulness and beastliness there is, you must square God with that. Or there is no universal God, but only a coldness, a vast cruel difference.

"I would not make my peace with such a God if I could....

"I tell you of these black and sinister realities, and what do you reply? That it is all right, because after death we shall get away from them. Why! if presently I go down under the surgeon's knife, down out of this hot and weary world, and then find myself being put together by a spirit doctor in this *beyond* of yours, waking up to a new world of amiable conversations and artificial flowers, having my hair restored and the gaps among my teeth filled up, I shall feel like someone who has deserted his kind, who has sneaked from a sick-room into a party.... Well— my infection will go with me. I shall talk of nothing but the tragedy out of which I have come which still remains— which continues— tragedy.

"And yet I believe in Immortality!"

Dr. Barrack, who had hitherto been following Mr. Huss with evident approval, started, sounded a note of surprise and protest, and fixed accusing eyes upon him. For the moment he did not interrupt.

"But it is not I that am immortal, but the God within me. All this personal immortality of which you talk is a mockery of our personalities. What is there personal in us that can live? What makes us our very selves? It is all a matter of little mean things, small differences, slight defects. Where does personal love grip?— on just these petty things.... Oh! dearly and bitterly did I love my son, and what is it that my heart most craves for now? Hi a virtues? No! His ambitions? His achievements?... No! none of these things.... But for a certain queer flush among his freckles, for a kind of high crack in his voice... a certain absurd hopefulness in his talk... the sound of his footsteps, a little halt there was in the rhythm of them. These are the things we long for. These are the things that wring the heart.... But all these things are just the mortal things, just the defects that would be touched out upon this higher plane you talk about. You would give him back to me smoothed and polished and regularized. So, I grant, it must be if there is to be this higher plane. But what does it leave of personal distinction? What does it leave of personal love?

"When my son has had his defects smoothed away, then he

will be like all sons. When the older men have been ironed out, they will be like the younger men. There is no personality in hope and honour and righteousness and truth.... My son has gone. He has gone for evermore. The pain may some day go ... The immortal thing in us is the least personal thing. It is not you nor I who go on living; it is Man that lives on, Man the Universal, and he goes on living, a tragic rebel in this same world and in no other...."

Mr. Huss leant back in his chair.

"There burns an undying fire in the hearts of men. By that fire I live. By that I know the God of my Salvation. His will is Truth; His will is Service. He urges me to conflict, without consolations, without rewards. He takes and does not restore. He uses up and does not atone. He suffers— perhaps to triumph, and we must suffer and find our hope of triumph in Him. He will not let me shut my eyes to sorrow, failure, or perplexity. Though the universe torment and slay me, yet will I trust in Him. And if He also must die— Nevertheless I can do no more; I must serve Him...."

He ceased. For some moments no one spoke, silenced by his intensity.

V. — ELIHU REPROVES JOB

§ 1

"I DON'T know how all this strikes you," said Mr. Farr, turning suddenly upon Dr. Barrack.

"Well— it's interesting" said Dr. Barrack, leaning forward upon his folded arms upon the table, and considering his words carefully.

"It's interesting" he repeated. "I don't know how far you want to hear what I think about it. I'm rather a downright person."

Sir Eliphaz with great urbanity motioned him to speak on.

"There's been, if you'll forgive me, nonsense upon both sides."

He turned to Sir Eliphaz. "This Spook stuff," he said, and paused and compressed his lips and shook his head.

"It won't do.

"I have given some little attention to the evidences in that matter. I'm something of a psychologist— a doctor has to be. Of course, Sir Eliphaz, you're not responsible for all the nonsense you have been talking about sublimated bricks and spook dogs made of concentrated smell..."

Sir Eliphaz was convulsed. "Tut, tut!" he said. "But indeed—!"

"No offence, Sir Eliphaz! If you don't want me to talk I won't; but if you do, then I must say what I have in my mind. And as I say, I don't hold you responsible for the things you have been saying. All this cheap medium stuff has been shot upon the world by Sir Oliver J. Lodge, handed out by him to people distraught with grief, in a great fat impressive-looking volume.... No end of them have tried their utmost to take it seriously.... It's been a pitiful business.... I've no doubt the man is honest after his lights, but what lights they are! Obstinate credulity posing as liberalism. He takes every pretence and dodge of these mediums, he accepts their explanations, he edits their babble and rearranges it to make it seem striking. Look at his critical ability! Because many of the mediums are fairly respectable people who either make no money by their— revelations, or at most a very ordinary living—it's a guinea a go, I believe, usually— he insists upon their honesty. That's his key blunder. Any doctor could tell him, as I could have told him after my first year's practice, that telling the truth is the very last triumph of the human mind. Hardly any of my patients tell the truth—ever. It isn't only that they haven't a tithe of the critical ability and detachment necessary, they haven't any real desire to tell the truth. They want to produce effects. Human beings are artistic still; they aren't beginning to be scientific. Either they minimize or they exaggerate. We all do. If I saw a cat run over outside and I came in here to tell you about it, I should certainly touch up the story, make it more dramatic, hurt the cat more, make the dray bigger and so on. I should want to justify my telling the story. Put a woman in that chair there, tell her to close her eyes and feel odd, and she'll feel odd right enough; tell her to produce words and sentences that she finds in her head and she'll produce them; give her half a hint that it comes from eastern Asia and the stuff will begin to correspond to her ideas of pigeon English. It isn't that she is cunningly and elaborately deceiving you. It is that she wants to come up to your expectation. You are focussing your interest on her, and all human beings like to have interest focussed on them, so long as it isn't too hostile. She'll cling to that interest all she knows how. She'll cling instinctively. Most of these mediums never held the attention of a roomful of people in their lives until they found out this way of doing it.... What can you expect?"

Dr. Barrack cleared his throat. "But all that's beside the question, " he said. "Don't think that because I reject all this spook stuff, I'm setting up any finality for the science we have to-day. It's just a little weak squirt of knowledge— all the science in the world. I grant you there may be forces, I would almost say there must be forces in the world, forces universally present, of which we still know nothing. Take the case of electricity. What did men know of electricity in the days of Gilbert? Practically nothing. In the early Neolithic age I doubt if any men had ever noticed there was such a thing as air. I grant you that most things are still unknown. Things perhaps right under our noses. But that doesn't help the case of Sir Eliphaz one little bit. These unknown things, as they become known, will join on to the things we do know. They'll complicate or perhaps simplify our ideas, but they won't contradict our general ideas. They'll be things in the system. They won't get you out of the grip of the arguments Mr. Huss has brought forward. So far, so far as concerns your Immortality, Sir Eliphaz, I am, you see, entirely with Mr. Huss. It's a fancy; it's a dream. As a fancy it's about as pretty as creaking boards at bedtime; as a dream—. It's unattractive. As Mr. Huss has said.

"But when it comes to Mr. Huss and his Immortality then I find myself with you, gentlemen. That too is a dream. Less than a dream. Less even than a fancy; it's a play on words. Here is this Undying Flame, this Spirit of God in man; it's in him, he says, it's in you, Sir Eliphaz, it's in you, Mr.— Dad, wasn't it? it's in this other gentleman whose name I didn't quite catch; and it's in me. Well, it's extraordinary that none of us know of it except Mr. Huss. How you feel about it I don't know, but personally I object to being made part of God and one with Mr. Huss without my consent in this way. I prefer to remain myself. That may be egotism, but I am by nature an egotistical creature. And Agnostic....

"You've got me talking now, and I may as well go through with it. What is an Agnostic really? A man who accepts fully the limitations of the human intelligence, who takes the world as he finds it, and who takes himself as he finds himself and declines to go further. There may be other universes and dimensions galore. There may be a fourth dimension, for example, and, if you like, a fifth dimension and a sixth dimension and any number of other dimensions. They don't concern me. I live in this universe and in three dimensions, and I have no more interest in all these other universes and dimensions than a bug under the wallpaper has in the deep, deep sea. Possibly there are bugs under the wallpaper with a kind of reasoned consciousness of the existence of the deep, deep sea, and a half belief that when at last the Keating's powder gets them, thither they will go. I— if I may have one more go at the image— just live under the wallpaper.

"I am an Agnostic, I say. I have had my eyes pretty well open at the universe since I came into it six and thirty years ago. And not only have I never seen nor heard of nor smelt nor touched a ghost or spirit, Sir Eliphaz, but I have never seen a gleam or sign of this Providence, the Great God of the World of yours, or of this other minor and modern God that Mr. Huss has taken up. In the hearts of men I have found malformations, ossifications, clots, and fatty degeneration; but never a God.

"You will excuse me if I speak plainly to you, gentlemen, but this gentleman, whose name I haven't somehow got—"

"Farr."

"Mr. Farr, has brought it down on himself and you. He called me in, and I am interested in these questions. It's clear to me that since we exist there's something in all this. But what it is I'm convinced I haven't the ganglia even to begin to understand. I decline either the wild guesses of the Spookist and Providentialist— I must put you there, I'm afraid, Sir Eliphaz or the metaphors of Mr. Huss. Fact...."

Dr. Barrack paused. "I put my faith in Fact."

"There's a lot in Fact," said Mr. Dad, who found much that was congenial in the doctor's downright style.

"What do I see about me?" asked Dr. Barrack. "A struggle for existence. About that I ask a very plain and simple question: why try to get behind it? That is It. It made me. I study it and watch it. It put me up like a cock-shy, and it keeps on trying to destroy me. I do my best to dodge its blows. It got my leg. My head is bloody but unbowed. I reproduce my kind— as abundantly as circumstances permit—I stamp myself upon the universe as much as possible. If I am right, if I do the right things and have decently good luck, I shall hold out until my waning instincts dispose me to rest. My breed and influence are the marks of my Tightness. What else is there? You may call this struggle what you like. God, if you like. But God for me is an anthropomorphic idea. Call it The Process."

"Why not Evolution?" said Mr. Huss.

"I prefer The Process. The word Evolution rather begs the moral question. It's a cheap word. 'Shon!' Evolution seems to suggest just a simple and automatic unfolding. The Process is complex; it has its ups and downs— as Mr. Huss understands. It is more like a Will than an Automaton. A Will feeling about. It isn't indifferent to us as Mr. Huss suggests; it uses us. It isn't subordinate to us as Sir Eliphaz would have us believe; playing the part of a Providence just for our comfort and happiness. Some of us are hammer and some of us are anvil, some of us are sparks and some of us are the beaten stuff which survives. The Process doesn't confide in us; why should it? We learn what we can about it, and make what is called a practical use of it, for that is what the will in the Process requires." Mr. Dad, stirred by the word 'practical,' made a noise of assent. But not a very confident noise: a loan rather than a gift.

"And that is where it seems to me Mr. Huss goes wrong altogether. He does not submit himself to those Realities. He sets up something called the Spirit in Man, or the God in his Heart, to judge them. He wants to judge the universe by the standards of the human intelligence at its present stage of development. That's where I fall out with him. These are not fixed standards. Man goes on developing and evolving. Some things offend the sense of justice in Mr. Huss, but that is no enduring criterion of justice; the human sense of justice has developed out of something different, and it will develop again into something different. Like everything else in us, it has been produced by the Process and it will be modified by the Process. Some things, again, he says are not beautiful. There also he would condemn. But nothing changes like the sense of beauty. A band of art students can start a new movement,

101

cubist, vorticist, or what not, and change your sense of beauty. If seeing things as beautiful conduces to survival, we shall see them as beautiful sooner or later, rest assured. I daresay the hyenas admire each other— in the rutting season anyhow.... So it is with mercy and with everything. Each creature has its own standards. After man is the Beyond-Man, who may find mercy folly, who may delight in things that pain our feeble spirits. We have to obey the Process in our own place and our own time. That is how I see things. That is the stark truth of the universe looked at plainly and hard."

The lips of Mr. Dad repeated noiselessly: "plainly and hard." But he felt very uncertain.

For some moments the doctor sat with his forearms resting on the table as if he had done. Then he resumed.

"I gather that this talk here to-day arose out of a discussion about education."

"You'd hardly believe it," said Mr. Dad.

But Dr. Barrack's next remark checked Mr. Dad's growing approval. "That seems perfectly logical to me. It's one of the things I can never understand about schoolmasters and politicians and suchlike, the way they seem to take it for granted you can educate and not bring in religion and socialism and all your beliefs. What *is* education? Teaching young people to talk and read and write and calculate in order that they may be told how they stand in the world and what we think we and the world generally are up to, and the part we expect them to play in the game. Well, how can we do that and at the same time leave it all out? What is the game? That is what every youngster wants to know. Answering him, is education. Either we are going to say what we think the game is plainly and straightforwardly, or else we are going to make motions as though we were educating when we are really doing nothing of the kind. In which case the stupid ones will grow up with their heads all in a muddle and be led by any old catchword anywhere according to luck, and the clever ones will grow up with the idea that life is a sort of empty swindle. Most educated people in this country believe it is a sham and a swindle. They flounder about and never get up against a reality.... It's amazing how people can lose their grip on reality— how most people have. The way my patients come along to me and tell me lies— even about their stomach-aches. The idea of anything being direct and reasonable has gone clean out of their heads. They think they can fool me about the facts, and that when I'm properly fooled, I shall then humbug their stomachs into not aching— somehow....

"Now my gospel is this:— face facts. Take the world as it is and take yourself as you are. And the fundamental fact we all have to face is this, that this Process takes no account of our desires or fears or moral ideas or anything of the sort. It puts us up, it tries us over, and if we don't stand the tests it knocks us down and ends us. That may not be right as you test it by your little human standards, but it is right by the atoms and the stars. Then what must a proper Education be?"

Dr. Barrack paused. "Tell them what the world is, tell them every rule and trick of the game mankind has learnt, and tell them 'Be yourselves.' Be yourselves up to the hilt. It is no good being anything but your essential self because—"

Dr. Barrack spoke like one who quotes a sacred formula. "*There is no inheritance of acquired characteristics.* Your essential self, your essential heredity, are on trial. Put everything of yourself into the Process. If the Process wants you it will accept you; if it doesn't you will go under. You can't help it—either way. You may be the bit of marble that is left in the statue, or you may be the bit of marble that is thrown away. You can't help it. *Be yourself!*"

Dr. Barrack had sat back; he raised his voice at the last words and lifted his hand as if to smite the table. But, so good a thing is professional training, he let his hand fall slowly, as he remembered that Mr. Huss was his patient.

§ 2

Mr. Huss did not speak for some moments. He was thinking so deeply that he seemed to be unobservant of the cessation of the doctor's discourse.

Then he awoke to the silence with a start.

"You do not differ among yourselves so much as you may think," he said at last.

"You all argue to one end, however wide apart your starting points may be. You argue that men may lead fragmentary lives....

"And," he reflected further, "submissive lives."

"*Not* submissive," said Dr. Barrack in a kind of footnote.

"You say, Sir Eliphaz, that this Universe is in the charge of Providence, all-wise and amiable. That He guides this world to ends we cannot understand; desirable ends, did we but know them, but incomprehensible; that this life, this whole Universe, is but the starting point for a developing series of immortal lives. And from this you conclude that the part a human being has to play in this scheme is the part of a trustful child, which need only not pester the Higher Powers, which need only do its few simple congenial duties, to be surely preserved and rewarded and carried on."

"There is much in simple faith," said Sir Eliphaz; "sneer though you may."

"But your view is a grimmer one, Dr. Barrack; you say that this Process is utterly beyond knowledge and control. We cannot alter it or appease it. It makes of some of us vessels of honour and of others vessels of dishonour. It has scrawled our race across the black emptiness of space, and it may wipe us out again. Such is the quality of Fate. We can but follow our lights and instincts.... In the end, in practical matters, your teaching marches with the teaching of Sir Eliphaz. You bow to the thing that is; he gladly and trustfully— with a certain old-world courtesy, you grimly—in the modern style...."

For some moments Mr. Huss sat with compressed lips, as though he listened to the pain within him. Then he said: "I don't.

"I don't submit. I rebel—not in my own strength nor by my own impulse. I rebel by the spirit of God in me. I rebel not merely to make weak gestures of defiance against the black disorder and cruelties of space and time, but for mastery. I am a rebel of pride— I am full of the pride of God in my heart. I am the servant of a rebellious and adventurous God who may yet bring order into this cruel and frightful chaos in which we seem to be driven hither and thither like leaves before the wind, a God who, in spite of all appearances, may yet rule over it at last and mould it to his will."

"*What* a world it will be!" whispered Mr. Farr, unable to restrain himself and yet half-ashamed of his sneer.

"What a world it is, Farr! What a cunning and watchful world! Does it serve even *you*? So insecure has it become that opportunity may yet turn a frightful face upon you— in the very moment as you snatch....

"But you see how I differ from you all. You see that the spirit of my life and of my teaching—of my teaching— for all its weaknesses and slips and failures, is a fight against that Dark Being of the universe who seeks to crush us all. Who broods over me now even as I talk to you.... It is a fight against disorder, a refusal of that very submission you have made, a repudiation altogether of that same voluntary death in life...."

He moistened his lips and resumed.

"The end and substance of all real education is to teach men and women of the Battle of God, to teach them of the beginnings of life upon this lonely little planet amidst the endless stars, and how those beginnings have unfolded; to show them how man has arisen through the long ages from amidst the beasts, and the nature of the struggle God wages through him, and to draw all men together out of themselves into one common life and effort with God. The nature of God's struggle is the essence of our dispute. It is a struggle, with a hope of victory but with no assurance. You have argued, Sir Eliphaz, that it is an unreal struggle, a sham fight, that indeed all things are perfectly adjusted and for our final happiness, and when I have reminded you a little of the unmasked horrors about us, you have shifted your ground of compensation into another— into an incredible— world."

Sir Eliphaz sounded dissent musically. Then he waved his long hand as Mr. Huss paused and regarded him. "But go on!" he said. "Go on!"

"And now I come to you, Dr. Barrack, and your modern fatalism. You hold this universe is uncontrollable— anyhow. And incomprehensible. For good or ill— we can be no more than our strenuous selves. You must, you say, *be yourself.* I answer, you must lose yourself in something altogether greater— in God.... There is a curious likeness, Doctor, and a curious difference in your views and mine. I think you see the world very much as I see it, but you see it coldly like a man before sunrise, and I—"

He paused. "There is a light upon it," he asserted with a noticeable flatness in his voice. "There is a light... light..."

He became silent. For a while it seemed as if the light he spoke of had gone from him and as if the shadow had engulfed him. When he spoke again it was with an evident effort.

He turned to Dr. Barrack. "You think," he said, "that there is a will in this Process of yours which will take things somewhere, somewhere definitely greater or better or onward. I hold that there is no will at all except in and through ourselves. If there be any will at all ... I hold that even your maxim 'be ourselves' is a paradox, for we cannot be ourselves until we have lost ourselves in God. I have talked to Sir Eliphaz and to you since you came in, of the boundless disorder and evil of nature. Let me talk to you now of the boundless miseries that arise from the disorderliness of men and that must continue age after age until either men are united in spirit and in truth or destroyed through their own incoherence. Whether men will be lost or saved I do not know. There have been times when I was sure that God would triumph in us.... But dark shadows have fallen upon my spirit....

"Consider the posture of men's affairs now, consider where

they stand today, because they have not yet begun to look deeply and frankly into realities; because, as they put it, they take life as they find it, because *they are themselves*, heedless of history, and do not realize that in truth they are but parts in one great adventure in space and time. For four years now the world has been marching deeper and deeper into tragedy.... Our life that seemed so safe grows insecure and more and more insecure.... Six million soldiers, six million young men, have been killed on the battlefields alone; three times as many have been crippled and mutilated; as many again who were not soldiers have been destroyed. That has been only the beginning of the disaster that has come upon our race. All human relationships have been strained; roads, ships, harvests destroyed; and behind the red swift tragedy of this warfare comes the gaunt and desolating face of universal famine now, and behind famine that inevitable follower of famine, pestilence. You gentlemen who have played so useful a part in supplying munitions of war, who have every reason in days well spent and energies well used to see a transitory brightness upon these sombre things, you may tell me that I lack faith when I say that I can see nothing to redeem the waste and destruction of the last four years and the still greater waste and spiritless disorder and poverty and disease ahead of us. You will tell me that the world has learnt a lesson it could learn in no other way, that we shall set up a World League of Nations now and put an end to war. But on what will you set up your World League of Nations? What foundations have you made in the last four years but ruins? Is there any common idea, any common understanding yet in the minds of men? They are still taking the world as they find it, they are being their unmitigated selves more than ever, and below the few who scramble for profits now is a more and more wolfish multitude scrambling for bread. There are no common ideas in men's minds upon which we can build. How can men be united except by common ideas? The schools have failed the world. What common thought is there in the world? A loud bawling of base newspapers, a posturing of politicians. You can see chaos coming again over all the east of Europe now, and bit by bit western Europe crumbles and drops into the confusion. Art, science, reasoned thought, creative effort, such things have ceased altogether in Russia; they may have ceased there perhaps for centuries; they die now in Germany; the universities of the west are bloodless and drained of their youth. That war that seemed at first so like the dawn of a greater age has ceased to matter in the face of this greater disaster. The French and British and Americans are beating back the Germans from Paris. Can they beat them back to any distance? Will not this present counterthrust diminish and fail as the others have done? Which side may first drop exhausted now, will hardly change the supreme fact. The supreme fact is exhaustion— exhaustion, mental as well as material, failure to grasp and comprehend, cessation even of attempts to grasp and comprehend, slackening of every sort of effort.

"What's the *good* of such despair?" said Mr. Dad.

"I do not despair. No. But what is the good of lying about hope and success in the midst of failure and gathering disaster? What is the good of saying that mankind wins— automatically—against the spirit of evil, when mankind is visibly losing point after point, is visibly losing heart? What is the good of pretending that there is order and benevolence or some sort of splendid and incomprehensible process in this festering waste, this windy desolation of tremendous things? There is no reason anywhere, there is no creation anywhere, except the undying fire, the spirit of God in the hearts of men... which may fail... which may fail... which seems to me to fail."

§ 3

He paused. Dr. Barrack cleared his throat.

"I don't want to seem obdurate," said Dr. Barrack. "I want to respect deep feeling. One must respect deep feeling.... But for the life of me I can't put much meaning into this phrase, *the spirit of God in the hearts of men*. It's rather against my habits to worry a patient, but this is so interesting— this is an exceptional occasion. I would like to ask you, Mr. Huss— frankly— is there anything very much more to it, than a phrase!"

There was no answer.

"Words," said Mr. Dad; " joost words. If Mr. Huss had ever spent three months of war time running a big engineering factory—"

"My mind is a sceptical mind," Dr. Barrack went on, after staring a moment to see if Mr. Dad meant to finish his sentence. "I want things I can feel and handle. I am an Agnostic by nature and habit and profession. A Doubting Thomas, born and bred. Well, I take it that about the universe Mr. Huss is very much of an Agnostic too. More so. He doubts more than I do. He doubts whether there is any trace of plan or purpose in it. What I call a Process, he calls a windy desolation. He sees Chaos still waiting for a creator. But then he sets up against that this undying fire of his, this spirit of God, which is lit in him and only waiting to be lighted in us, a sort of insurgent apprentice creator. Well—"

The doctor frowned and meditated on his words.

"I want more of the practical outcome of this fire. I admit a certain poetry in the idea, but I am a plain and practical man. Give me something to know this fire by and to recognize it again when I see it. I won't ask *why* 'undying.' I won't quibble about that. But what does this undying fire mean in actual things and our daily life? In some way it is mixed up with teaching history in schools." A faint note of derision made him glance at the face to his right. "That doesn't strike me as being so queer as it seems to strike Mr. Farr. It interests me. There is a cause for it. But I think there are several links Mr. Huss hasn't shown and several vital points he still has to explain. This undying fire is something that is burning in Mr. Huss, and I gather from his pretty broad hints it ought, he thinks, to be burning in me— and you, gentlemen. It is something that makes us forget our little personal differences, makes us forget ourselves, and brings us all into line against— what. That's my first point;—against what? I don't see the force and value of this line-up. *I* think we struggle against one another by nature and necessity; that we polish one another in the struggle and sharpen our edges. I think that out of this struggle for existence comes better things and better. They may not be better things by our standards now, but by the standards of the Process, they are. Sometimes the mills of the Process may seem overpoweringly grim and high and pitiless; that is a question of scale. But Mr. Huss does not believe in the struggle. He wants to take men's minds and teach them so that they will not struggle against each other but live and work all together. *For* what? That is my second point;— *for what?* There is a rationality in my idea of an everlasting struggle making incessantly for betterment, such an idea does at any rate give a direction and take us somewhere; but there is no rationality in declaring we are still fighting and fighting more than ever, while in effect we are arranging to stop that struggle which carries life on— if we can— if we can.

That is the paradox of Mr. Huss. When there is neither competition at home nor war abroad, when the cat and the bird have come to a satisfactory understanding, when the spirit of his human God rules even in the jungle and the sea, then where shall we be heading? Time will be still unfolding. But man will have halted. If he has ceased to compete individually he will have halted. Mr. Huss looks at me as if he thought I wronged him in saying that. Well, then he must answer my questions; what will the Human God be leading us against, and what shall we be living *for*?"

§ 4

"Let me tell you first what the spirit of God struggles against," said Mr. Huss.

"I will not dispute that this Process of yours has made good things; all the good things in man it has made as well as all the evil. It has made them indifferently. In us—in some of us—it has made the will to seize upon that chance-born good and separate it from the chance-born evil. The spirit of God rises out of your process as if he were a part of your process.... Except for him, the good and evil are inextricably mixed; good things flower into evil things and evil things wholly or partially redeem themselves by good consequences. 'Good' and 'evil' have meaning only for us. The Process is indifferent; it makes, it destroys, it favours, it torments. On its own account it preserves nothing and continues nothing. It is just careless. But for us it has made opportunity. Life is opportunity. Unless we do now ourselves seize hold upon life and the Process while we are in it, the Process, becoming uncontrollable again, will presently sweep us altogether away. In the back of your mind, doctor, is the belief in a happy ending just as much as in the mind of Sir Eliphaz. I see deeper because I am not blinded by health. You think that beyond man comes some sort of splendid super-man. A healthy delusion! There is nothing beyond man unless men will that something shall be. We shall be wiped out as carelessly as we have been made, and something else will come, as disconnected and aimless, something neither necessarily better nor necessarily worse but something different, to be wiped out in its turn. Unless the spirit of God that moves in us can rouse us to seize this universe for Him and ourselves, that is the nature of your Process. Your Process is just Chaos; man is the opportunity, the passing opportunity for order in the waste.

"People write and talk as if this great war which is now wrecking the world, was a dramatic and consecutive thing. They talk of it as a purge, as a great lesson, as a phase in history that marks the end of wars and divisions. So it might be; but is it so and will it be so? I asked you a little time ago to look straightly at the realities of animal life, of life in general as we know it. I think I did a little persuade you to my own sense of shallowness of our assumption that there is any natural happiness. The poor beasts and creatures have to suffer. I ask you now to look as straightly at the things that men have done and endured in this war. It is plain that they have shown extraordinary fertility and ingenuity in the inventions they have used and an amazing capacity for sacrifice and courage; but it is, I argue, equally plain that the pains and agonies they have undergone have taught the race little or nothing, and that their devices have been mainly for their own destruction. The only lesson and the only betterment that can come out of this war will come if men, inspired by the Divine courage, say ' This and all such things must end.'... "But I do not perceive them saying that. On the other hand I do perceive a great amount of human energy and ability that has been devoted and is still being devoted to things that lead straight to futility and extinction.

"The most desolating thing about this war is neither the stupidity nor the cruelty of it, but the streak of perversion that has run through it. Against the meagreness of the intelligence that made the war, against the absolute inability of the good forces in life to arrest it and end it, I ask you to balance the intelligence and devotion that has gone to such an enterprise as the offensive use of poison gas. Consider the ingenuity and the elaboration of that; the different sorts of shell used, the beautifully finished devices to delay the release of the poison so as to catch men unawares after their gas masks are removed. One method much in favour with the Germans now involves the use of two sorts of gas. They have a gas now not very deadly but so subtle that it penetrates the gas masks and produces nausea and retching. The man is overcome by the dread of being sick so that he will clog his mask and suffocate, and he snatches off his protection in an ungovernable physical panic. Then the second gas, of the coarser, more deadly type, comes into play. That he breathes in fully. His breath catches; he realizes what he has done but it is too late; death has him by the throat; he passes through horrible discomfort and torment to the end. You cough, you stagger, you writhe upon the ground and are deadly sick.... You die heaving and panting, with staring eyes.... So it is men are being killed now; it is but one of a multitude of methods, disgusting, undignified, and monstrous, but intelligent, technically admirable.... You cannot deny, Doctor Barrack, that this ingenious mixture is one of the last fruits of your Process. To that your Process has at last brought men from the hoeing and herding of Neolithic days.

"Now tell me how is the onward progress of mankind to anything, anywhere, secured by this fine flower of the Process? Intellectual energy, industrial energy, are used up without stint to make this horror possible; multitudes of brave young men are spoilt or killed. Is there any selection in it? Along such lines can you imagine men or life or the universe getting anywhere at all?

"Why do they do such things?

"They do not do it out of a complete and organized impulse to evil. If you took the series of researches and inventions that led at last to this use of poison gas, you would find they were the work of a multitude of mainly amiable, fairly virtuous, and kindly-meaning men. Each one was *doing his bit*, as Mr. Dad would say; each one, to use your phrase, doctor, was *being himself* and utilizing the gift that was in him in accordance with the drift of the world about him; each one, Sir Eliphaz, was modestly *taking the world as he found it*. They were living in an uninformed world with no common understanding and no collective plan, a world ignorant of its true history and with no conception of its future. Into these horrors they drifted for the want of a world education. Out of these horrors no lesson will be learnt, no will can arise, for the same reason. Every man lives ignorantly in his own circumstances, from hand to mouth, from day to day, swayed first of all by this catchword and then by that.

"Let me take another instance of the way in which human ability and energy if they are left to themselves, without co-ordination, without a common basis of purpose, without a God, will run into cul-de-sacs of mere horribleness; let me remind you a little of what the submarine is and what it signifies. In this country we think of the submarine as an instrument of murder; but we think of it as something ingeniously contrived and at any rate not tormenting and destroying the hands that guide it. I will not recall to you the stories that fill our newspapers of men drowning in the night, of crowded boatloads of sailors and passengers shelled and sunken, of men forced to clamber out of the sea upon the destroying U-boat and robbed of their lifebelts in order that when it submerged they should be more surely drowned. I want you to think of the submarine in itself. There is a kind of crazy belief that killing, however cruel, has a kind of justification in the survival of the killer; we make that our excuse for instance for the destruction of the native Tasmanians who were shot whenever they were seen, and killed by poisoned meat left in their paths. But the marvel of these submarines is that they also torture and kill their own crews. They are miracles of short-sighted ingenuity for the common unprofitable reasonless destruction of Germans and their enemies. They are almost quintessential examples of the elaborate futility and horror into which partial ideas about life, combative and competitive ideas of life, thrust mankind.

"Take some poor German boy with an ordinary sort of intelligence, an ordinary human disposition to kindliness, and some gallantry, who becomes finally a sailor in one of these craft. Consider his case and what we do to him. You will find in him a sample of what we are doing for mankind. As a child he is ingenuous, teachable, plastic. He is also egotistical, greedy, and suspicious. He is easily led and easily frightened. He likes making things if he knows how to make them; he is capable of affection and capable of resentment. He is a sheet of white paper upon which anything may be written. His parents teach him, his companions, his school. Do they teach him anything of the great history of mankind? Do they teach him of his blood brotherhood with all men? Do they tell him anything of discovery, of exploration, of human effort and achievement? No. They teach him that he belongs to a blonde and wonderful race, the only race that matters on this planet. (No such distinct race ever existed; it is a lie for the damning of men.) And these teachers incite him to suspicion and hatred and contempt of all other races. They fill his mind with fears and hostilities. Everything German they tell him is good and splendid. Everything not German is dangerous and wicked. They take that poor actor of an emperor at Potsdam and glorify him until he shines upon this lad's mind like a star....

"The boy grows up a mental cripple; his capacity for devotion and self- sacrifice is run into a mould of fanatical loyalty for the Kaiser and hatred for foreign things. Comes this war, and the youngster is only too eager to give himself where he is most needed. He is told that the submarine war is the sure way of striking the enemies of his country a conclusive blow. To be in a submarine is to be at the spear point. He dare scarcely hope that he will be accepted for this vital service; to which princes might aspire. But he is fortunate; he is. He trains for a submarine.

"I do not know how far you gentlemen remember your youth. A schoolmaster perhaps remembers more of his early adolescence than other men because he is being continually reminded of it. But it is a time of very fine emotions, boundless ambitions, a newly awakened and eager sense of beauty. This youngster sees himself as a hero, fighting for his half-divine Kaiser, for dear Germany, against the cold and evil barbarians who resist and would destroy her. He passes through his drill and training. He goes down into a submarine for the first time, clambers down the narrow hatchway. It is a little cold, but wonderful; a marvellous machine. How can such a nest of inventions, ingenuities, beautiful metal-work, wonderful craftsmanship, be anything but right! His mind is full of dreams of proud enemy battleships smitten and heeling over into the waters, while he watches his handiwork with a stern pride, a restrained exultation, a sense of Germany vindicated....

"That is how his mind has been made for him. That is the sort of mind that has been made and is being made in boys all over the world.... Because there is no common plan in the world, because each person in the making of this boy, just as each person in the making of the submarine, had 'been himself' and 'done his bit,' followed his own impulses and interests without regard to the whole, regardless of any plan or purpose in human affairs, ignorant of the spirit of God who would unify us and lead us to a common use for all our gifts and energies.

"Let me go on with the story of this youngster....

"Comes a day when he realizes the reality of the work he is doing for his kind. He stands by one of the guns of the submarine in an attack upon some wretched ocean tramp. He realizes that the war he wages is no heroic attack on pride or predominance, but a mere murdering of traffic. He sees the little ship shelled, the wretched men killed and wounded, no tyrants of the seas but sailormen like himself; he sees their boats smashed to pieces. Mostly such sinkings are done at dawn or sundown, under a level light which displays a world of black lines and black silhouettes asway with the slow heaving and falling of coldly shining water. These little black things, he realizes incredulously, that struggle and disappear amidst the wreckage are the heads of men, brothers to himself....

"For hundreds of thousands of men who have come into this war expecting bright and romantic and tremendous experiences their first killing must have been a hideous disillusionment. For none so much as for the men of the submarines. All that sense of being right and fine that carries men into battle, that carries most of us through the world, must have vanished completely at this first vision of reality. Our man must have asked himself, *'What am I doing?'*...

"In the night he must have lain awake and stared at that question in horrible doubt....

"We scold too much at the German submarine crews in this country. Most of us in their places would be impelled to go on as they go on. The work they do has been reached step by step, logically, inevitably, because our world has been content to drift along on false premises and haphazard assumptions about nationality and race and the order of things. These things have happened because the technical education of men has been better than their historical and social education. Once men have lost touch with, or failed to apprehend that idea of a single human community, that idea which is the substance of all true history and the essential teaching of God, it is towards such organized abominations as these that they drift— necessarily. People in this country who are just as incoherent in their minds, just as likely to drift into some kindred cul-de-sac of conduct, would have these U-boat men tortured— to show the superiority of their own moral standards.

"But indeed these men *are* tortured....

"Bear yet a little longer with this boy of mine in the U-boat. I've tried to suggest him to you with his conscience scared— at a moment when his submarine had made a kill. But those moments are rare. For most of its time the U-boat is under water and a hunted thing. The surface swarms with hostile craft; sea-planes and observation balloons are seeking it. Every time a U-boat comes even near to the surface it may be spotted by a sea-plane and destruction may fall upon it. Even when it is submerged below the limits of visibility in the turbid North Sea waters, the noise of its engines will betray it to a listening apparatus and a happy guess with a depth charge may end its career. I want you to think of the daily life of this youngster under these conditions. I want you to see exactly where wrong ideas, not his, but wrong ideas ruling in the world about him, are driving him.

"The method of detection by listening apparatus improves steadily, and nowadays our destroyers will follow up a U-boat sometimes for sixty or seventy hours, following her sounds as a hound follows the scent of its quarry. At last, if the U-boat cannot shake off her pursuers she must come to the surface and fight or surrender. That is the strangest game of Blind-Man that ever human beings played. The U-boat doubles and turns, listening also for the sounds of the pursuers at the surface. Are they coming nearer! Are they getting fainter? Unless a helpful mud-bank is available for it to lie up in silence for a time, the U-boat must keep moving and using up electrical force, so that ultimately it must come to the surface to recharge its batteries. As far as possible the crew of the U-boat are kept in ignorance of the chase in progress. They get hints from the anxiety or irritation of the commander, or from the haste and variety of his orders. Something is going on— they do not know quite what—something that may end disagreeably. If the pursuer tries a depth charge, then they know for certain from the concussion that the hand of death is feeling for them in the darkness.... "Always the dread of a depth charge must haunt the imagination of the U-boat sailor. Without notice, at any hour, may come thud and concussion to warn him that the destroying powers are on his track. The fragile ship jumps and quivers from end to end; the men are thrown about. That happens to our youngster. He curses the damned English. And if you think it over, what else can you expect him to curse? A little nearer and the rivets will start and actual leakage begin, letting in a pressure of several atmospheres. Yet a little nearer and the water will come pressing in through cracks and breaches at a score of points, the air will be compressed in his lungs, the long death struggle of the U-boat will begin, and after some hours of hopeless suffering he will suffocate and drown like a rat in a flooded tunnel....

"Think of the life of endless apprehension in that confined space below the waters. The air is almost always stuffy and sometimes it is poisonous. All sorts of evil chances may occur in this crowded tinful of machinery to release oppressive gases and evil odours. A whiff of chlorine for instance may warn the crew of flooded accumulators. At the first sting of chlorine the U-boat must come up at any risk.... And nothing can be kept dry. The surfaces of the apparatus and the furniture sweat continually; except where the machinery radiates a certain heat a clammy chill pervades the whole contrivance. Have you ever seen the thick blubber of a whale? Only by means of that enormous layer of non-conductor can a whale keep its body warm in spite of the waters about it. A U-boat cannot afford any layer of blubber. It is at the temperature of the dark under-waters. And this life of cold, fear, suffocation, headache and nausea is not sustained by hot and nourishing food. There is no blazing galley fire for the cook of the U-boat.

"The U-boat rolls very easily; she is, of course, no heavier nor lighter than the water in which she floats, and if by chance she touches bottom in shallow water, she bounds about like a rubber ball on a pavement. Inside the sailors are thrown about and dashed against the machinery.

"That is the quality of everyday life in a U-boat retained below the surface. Now think what an emergence involves. Up she comes until the periscope can scrutinize the sky and the nearer sea. Nothing in sight? Thank God! She rises out of the water and some of the sailors get a breath of fresh air. Not all, for there is no room nor time for all of them to come out. But the fortunate ones who get to the hatches may even have the luck of sunshine. To come to the surface on a calm open sea away from any traffic at all is the secret hope of every U-boat sailor. But suppose now there is something in sight. Then the U-boat must come up with infinite discretion and examine the quarry. It looks an innocent craft, a liner, a trawler, a cargo-boat. But is that innocence certain? How does the U-boat man know that she hasn't a gun? What new contrivance of the hunter may not hide behind that harmless-looking mask? Until they have put a ship down, the U-boat sailors never know what ugly surprise she may not have in store for them. When they approach a vessel they must needs be ignorant of what counter-attack creeps upon them from her unseen other side. As a consequence these men are in terror of every ship they hail.

"Is it any wonder then if their behaviour is hasty and hysterical, if they curse and insult the wretched people they are proposing to drown, if they fire upon them unexpectedly and do strange and abominable things? The U-boat man is no fine captain on his quarter deck. He is a man who lives a life of intense physical hardship and extreme fear, who faces overwhelming risks, in order to commit as inglorious a crime as any man can commit. He is a man already in hell.

"The Germans do what they can to keep up the spirit of these crews. An English captain who spent a fortnight upon one as a prisoner and who was recently released by way of Switzerland, says that when they had sunk a merchant ship 'they played victory music on the gramophone.' Imagine that bleak festival!

"The inevitable end of the U-boat sailor, unless he is lucky enough to get captured, is death, and a very horrible and slow death indeed. Sooner or later it is bound to come. Some never return from their first voyage. There is a brief spree ashore if they do; then out they go again. Perhaps they return a second time, perhaps not. Some may even have made a score of voyages, but sooner or later they are caught. The average life of a U-boat is less than five voyages— out and home. Of the crews of the original U-boats which began the U-boat campaign very few men survive to-day. When our young hopeful left his home in Germany to join the U-boat service, he left it for a certain death. He learns that slowly from the conversation of his mates. Men are so scarce now for this vile work that once Germany has got a man she will use him to the end.

"And that end—?

"I was given some particulars of the fate of one U-boat that were told by two prisoners who died at Harwich the other day. This particular boat was got by a mine which tore a hole in her aft. She was too disabled to come to the surface, and she began to sink tail down. Now the immediate effect of a hole in a U-boat is of course to bring the air pressure within her to the same level as the pressure of the water outside. For every ten yards of depth this means an addition of fourteen pounds to the square inch. The ears and blood vessels are suddenly subjected to this enormous pressure. There is at once a violent pain in the ears and a weight on the chest. Cotton wool has to be stuffed into ears and nostrils to save the ear drum. Then the boat is no longer on an even keel. The men stand and slip about on the sides of things. They clamber up the floor out of the way of the slowly rising water. For the water does not come rushing in to drown them speedily. It cannot do that because there is no escape for the air; the water creeps in steadily and stealthily as the U-boat goes deeper and deeper. It is a process of slow and crushing submergence that has the cruel deliberation of some story by Edgar Allan Poe; it may last for hours. A time comes when the lights go out and the rising waters stop the apparatus for keeping up the supply of oxygen and absorbing the carbonic acid. Suffocation begins. Think of what must happen in the minds of the doomed men crowded together amidst the machinery. In the particular case these prisoners described, several of the men drowned themselves deliberately in the rising waters inside the boat. And in another case where the boat was recovered full of dead men, they had all put their heads under the water inside the boat. People say the U-boat men carry poison against such mischances as this. They don't. It would be too tempting.

"When it becomes evident that the U-boat can never recover the surface, there is usually an attempt to escape by the hatches. The hatches can be opened when at last the pressure inside is equal to that of the water without. The water of course rushes in and sinks the U-boat to the bottom like a stone, but the men *who are nearest to the hatch* have a chance of escaping with the rush of air to the surface. There is of course a violent struggle to get nearest to the hatch. This is what happened in the case of the particular U-boat from which these prisoners came. The forward hatch was opened. Our patrol boat cruising above saw the waters thrown up by the air-burst and then the heads of the men struggling on the surface. Most of these men were screaming with pain. All of them went under before they could be picked up except two. And these two died in a day or so. They died because coming suddenly up to the ordinary atmosphere out of the compressed air of the sinking submarine had burst the tissues of their lungs. They were choked with blood.

"Think of those poor creatures dying in the hospital. They were worn out by fits of coughing and haemorrhage, but there must have been moments of exhausted quiet before the end, when our youngster lay and stared at the bleak walls of the ward and thought; when he asked himself, 'What have I been doing? What have I done? What has this world done for me? It has made me a murderer. It has tortured me and wasted me.... And I meant well by it....'

"Whether he thought at all about the making of the submarine, the numberless ingenuities and devices, the patience and devotion, that had gone to make that grim trap in which he had been caught at last, I cannot guess.... Probably he took it as a matter of course....

"So it was that our German youngster who dreamt dreams, who had ambitions, who wished to serve and do brave and honourable things, died.... So five thousand men at least have died, English some of them as well as German, in lost submarines beneath the waters of the narrow seas....

"There is a story and a true story. It is more striking than the fate of most men and women in the world, but is it, in its essence, different? Is not the whole life of our time in the vein of this story? Is not this story of youth and hope and possibility misled, marched step by step into a world misconceived, thrust into evil, and driven down to ugliness and death, only a more vivid rendering of what is now the common fate of great multitudes? Is there any one of us who is not in some fashion aboard a submarine, doing evil and driving towards an evil end?...

"What are the businesses in which men engage? How many of them have any likeness to freighted ships that serve the good of mankind? Think of the lying and cornering, the crowding and outbidding, the professional etiquette that robs the common man, the unfair advantage smugly accepted! What man among us can say, 'All that I do is service'? Our holding and our effort: is it much better than the long interludes below the surface, and when we come up to struggle for our own hands, torpedoing competitors, wrecking antagonists, how is it with us? The submarine sailors stare in the twilight at drowning men. Every day I stare at a world drowning in poverty and ignorance, a world awash in the seas of hunger, disease, and misery. We have been given leisure, freedom, and intelligence; what have we done to prevent these things?

"I tell you all the world is a submarine, and every one of us is something of a U-boat man. These fools who squeal in the papers for cruelties to the U-boat men do not realize their own part in the world.... We might live in sunshine and freedom and security, and we live cramped and cold, in bitter danger, because we are at war with our fellow men....

"But there, doctor, you have the answer to the first part of your question. You asked what the Spirit of God in Man was against. It is against these mental confusions, these ignorances, that thrust life into a frightful cul-de-sac, that the God in our Hearts urges us to fight.... He is crying out in our hearts to save us from these blind alleys of selfishness, darkness, cruelty, and pain in which our race must die; he is crying for the high road which is salvation, he is commanding the organized unity of mankind."

§ 5

The lassitude that had been earlier apparent in the manner of Mr. Huss had vanished. He was talking now with more energy; his eyes were bright and there was a flush in his cheeks. His voice was low, but his speech was clear and no longer broken by painful pauses.

"But your question had a double edge," he continued; " you asked me not only what it is that the Spirit of God in us fights against, but what it is he fights for. Whither does the high road lead 1? I have told you what I think the life of man is, a felted and corrupting mass of tragic experiences; let me tell you now a little, if this pain at my side will still permit it, what life upon this earth, under the leadership of the Spirit of God our Captain, might be.

"I will take it that men are still as they are, that all this world is individually the same; I will suppose no miraculous change in human nature; but I will suppose that events in the past have run along different channels, so that there has been much more thinking, much more exchange of thought, far better teaching. I want simply this world better taught, so that wherever the flame of God can be lit it has been lit. Everyone I will suppose *educated*. By *educated*, to be explicit, I mean a knowledge and understanding of history. Yes, Mr. Farr—salvation by history. Everyone about the earth I will suppose has been taught not merely to read and write and calculate, but has been given all that can be told simply and plainly of the past history of the earth, of our place in space and time, and the true history of mankind. I will not suppose that there is any greater knowledge of things than men actually possess to-day, but instead of its being confusedly stored in many minds and many books and many languages, it has all been sorted out and set out plainly so that it can be easily used. It has been kept back from no one, mistold to no one. Moreover I will suppose that instead of a myriad of tongues and dialects, all men can read the same books and talk together in the same speech.

"These you may say are difficult suppositions, but they are

not impossible suppositions. Quite a few resolute men could set mankind definitely towards such a state of affairs so that they would reach it in a dozen generations or so. But think what a difference there would be from our conditions in such a world. In a world so lit and opened by education, most of these violent dissensions that trouble mankind would be impossible. Instead of men and communities behaving like fever patients in delirium, striking at their nurses, oversetting their food and medicine and inflicting injuries on themselves and one another, they would be alive to the facts of their common origin, their common offspring— for at last in our descendants all our lives must meet again— and their common destiny. In that more open and fresher air, the fire that is God will burn more brightly, for most of us who fail to know God fail through want of knowledge. Many more men and women will be happily devoted to the common work of mankind, and the evil that is in all of us will be more plainly seen and more easily restrained. I doubt if any man is altogether evil, but in this dark world the good in men is handicapped and sacrifice is mocked. Bad example finishes what weak and aimless teaching has begun. This is a world where folly and hate can bawl sanity out of hearing. Only the determination of schoolmasters and teachers can hope to change that. How can you hope to change it by anything but teaching? Cannot you realize what teaching means!...

"When I ask you to suppose a world instructed and educated in the place of this old traditional world of unguided passion and greed and meanness and mean bestiality, a world taught by men instead of a world neglected by hirelings, I do not ask you to imagine any miraculous change in human nature. I ask you

129

only to suppose that each mind has the utmost enlightenment of which it is capable instead of its being darkened and overcast. Everyone is to have the best chance of being his best self. Everyone is to be living in the light of the acutest self-examination and the clearest mutual criticism. Naturally we shall be living under infinitely saner and more helpful institutions. Such a state of things will not indeed mitigate natural vanity or natural self-love; it will not rob the greedy man of his greed, the fool of his folly, the eccentric of his abnormality, nor the lustful of his lust. But it will rob them of excuses and hiding places; it will light them within and cast a light round about them; it will turn their evil to the likeness of a disease of which they themselves in their clear moments will be ready to be cured and which they will hesitate to transmit. That is the world which such of us schoolmasters and teachers among us as have the undying fire of God already lit in our hearts, do now labour, generation by generation, against defeat and sometimes against hope, to bring about; that is the present work God has for us. And as we do bring it about then the prospect opens out before mankind to a splendour....

"In this present world men live to be themselves; having their lives they lose them; in the world that we are seeking to make they will give themselves to the God of Mankind, and so they will live indeed. They will as a matter of course change their institutions and their methods so that all men may be used to the best effect, in the common work of mankind. They will take ' this little planet which has been torn into shreds of possession, and make it again one garden.

"The most perplexing thing about men at the present time is their lack of understanding of the vast possibilities of power and happiness that science is offering them—"

"Then why not teach *science*?" cried Mr. Farr.

"Provided only that they will unite their efforts. They solve the problems of material science in vain until they have solved their social and political problems. When those are solved, the mechanical and technical difficulties are trivial. It is no occult secret; it is a plain and demonstrable thing to-day that the world could give ample food and ample leisure to every human being, if only by a world-wide teaching the spirit of unity could be made to prevail over the impulse to dissension. And not only that, but it would then be possible to raise the common health and increase the common fund of happiness immeasurably. Look plainly at the world as it is. Most human beings when they are not dying untimely, are suffering more or less from avoidable disorders, they are ill or they are convalescent, or they are suffering from or crippled by some preventable taint in the blood, or they are stunted or weakened by a needlessly bad food supply, or spiritless and feeble through bad housing, bad clothing, dull occupations, or insecurity and anxiety. Few enjoy for very long stretches at a time that elementary happiness which is the natural accompaniment of sound health. This almost universal lowness of tone, which does not distress us only because most of us are unable to imagine anything better, means an enormous waste of human possibility; less work, less hopefulness. Isolated efforts will never raise men out of this swamp of malaise. At Woldingstanton we have had the best hygienic arrangements we could find, we have taken the utmost precautions, and yet there has scarcely been a year when our work has not been crippled and delayed by some epidemic, influenza one year, measles another, and so on. We take our precautions j but the townspeople, especially in the poorer quarters, don't and can't. I think myself the wastage of these perennial petty pestilences is far greater than that caused by the big epidemics that sometimes sweep the world. But all such things, great or petty, given a sufficient world unanimity, could be absolutely banished from human life. Given a sufficient unanimity and intelligent direction, men could hunt down all these infectious diseases, one by one, to the regions in which they are endemic, and from which they start out again and again to distress the world, and could stamp them out for ever. It is not want of knowledge prevents this now but want of a properly designed education, which would give people throughout the world the understanding, the confidence, and the will needed for so collective an enterprise.

"The sufferings and mutual cruelties of animals are no doubt a part of the hard aimlessness of nature, but men are in a position to substitute aim for that aimlessness, they have already all the knowledge and all the resources needed to escape from these cul-de-sacs of wrong-doing and suffering and ugly futility into which they jostle one another. But they do not do it because they have not been sufficiently educated and are not being sufficiently educated to sane understanding and effort. The bulk of their collective strength is dissipated in miserable squabbles and suspicions, in war and the preparation for war, in lawsuits and bickering, in making little sterile private hoards of wealth and power, in chaffering, in stupid persecutions and oppositions and vanities. It is not only that they live in a state of general infection and ill health and bad temper, ill nourished, ill housed and morally horrible, when the light is ready to shine upon them and health and splendour is within their grasp, but that all that they could so attain would be but the prelude to still greater attainments.

"Apart from and above the sweeping away of the poverty, filthiness and misery of life that would follow on an intelligent use of such powers and such qualities as men possess now, there would be a tremendous increase in happiness due to the contentment of belonging to one common comprehensible whole, of knowing that one played a part and a worthy part in an immortal and universal task. The merest handful of people can look with content upon the tenor of their lives to-day. A few teachers are perhaps aware that they serve God rightly, a few scientific investigators, a few doctors and bridge- builders and makers of machinery, a few food-growers and sailors and the like. They can I believe that they do something that is necessary, or build something which will endure. But most men and women to-day are like beasts caught in a tunnel; they follow base occupations, they trade and pander and dispute; there is no peace in their hearts; they gratify their lusts and seek excitements; they know they spend their lives in vain and they have no means of escape. The world is full of querulousness and abuse, derision and spite, mean tricks and floundering effort, vice without a gleam of pleasure and vain display, because blind Nature spews these people into being and there is no light to guide their steps. Yet there is work to be done by everyone, a plain reason for that work, and happiness in the doing of it....

"I do not know if any of us realize all that a systematic organization of the human intelligence upon the work of research would mean for our race. People talk of the wonders that scientific work has given us in the past two hundred years, wonders of which for the most part we are too disordered and foolish to avail ourselves fully. But what scientific research has produced so far must be as yet only the smallest earnest of what scientific research can presently give mankind. All the knowledge that makes to-day different from the world of Queen Elizabeth has been the work of a few score thousand men, mostly poorish men, working with limited material and restricted time, in a world that discouraged and misunderstood them. Many hundreds of thousands of men with gifts that would have been of the profoundest value in scientific work, have missed the education or the opportunity to use those gifts. But in a world clarified by understanding, the net of research would miss few of its born servants, there would be the swiftest, clearest communication of results from worker to worker, the readiest honour and help for every gift. Poor science, which goes about now amidst our crimes and confusions like an ill-trimmed evil-smelling oil lantern in a dark cavern in which men fight and steal, her flickering light, snatched first by this man and then by that, as often as not a help to violence and robbery, would become like the sunrise of a bright summer morning. We do not realize what in a little while mankind could do. Our power over matter, our power over life, our power over ourselves, would increase year by year and day by day.

"Here am I, after great suffering, waiting here for an uncertain operation that may kill me. *It need not have been so.* Here are we all, sitting hot and uncomfortable in this ill-ventilated, ill-furnished room, looking out upon a vile waste. *It need not have been so.* Such is the quality of our days. I sit here wrung by pain, in the antechamber of death, because mankind has suffered me to suffer.... All this could have been avoided.... Not for ever will such things endure, not for ever will the Mocker of

Mankind prevail....

"And such knowledge and power and beauty as we poor watchers before the dawn can guess at, are but the beginning of all that could arise out of these shadows and this torment. Not for ever shall life be marooned upon this planet, imprisoned by the cold and incredible emptiness of space. Is it not plain to you all, from what man in spite of everything has achieved, that he is but at the beginning of achievement? That presently he will take his body and his life and mould them to his will, that he will take gladness and beauty for himself as a girl will pick a flower and twine it in her hair. You have said, Doctor Barrack, that when industrial competition ends among men all change in the race will be at an end. But you said that unthinkingly. For when a collective will grows plain, there will be no blind thrusting into life and no blind battle to keep in life, like the battle of a crowd crushed into a cul-de-sac, any more. The qualities that serve the great ends of the race will be cherished and increased; the sorts of men and women that have these qualities least will be made to understand the necessary restraints of their limitation. You said that when men ceased to compete, they would stand still. Rather is it true that when men cease their internecine war, then and then alone can the race sweep forward. The race will grow in power and beauty swiftly, in every generation it will grow, and not only the human race. All this world will man make a garden for himself, ruling not only his kind but all the lives that live, banishing the cruel from life, making the others merciful and tame beneath his hand. The flies and mosquitoes, the thorns and poisons, the fungus in the blood, and the murrain upon his beasts, he will utterly end. He will rob the atoms of their energy and the depths of space of their secrets. He will break his prison in space. He will step from star to star as now we step from stone to stone across a stream. Until he stands in the light of God's presence and looks his Mocker and the Adversary in the face...."

"Oh! *Ravins!*" Mr. Dad burst out, unable to contain himself.

"You may think my mind is fevered because my body is in pain; but never was my mind clearer than it is now. It is as if I stood already half out of this little life that has held me so long. It is not a dream I tell, but a reality. The world is for man, the stars in their courses are for man— if only he will follow the God who calls to him and take the gift God offers. As I sit here and talk of these things to you here, they become so plain to me that I cannot understand your silence and why you do not burn— as I burn— with the fire of God's purpose...."

He stopped short. He seemed to have come to the end of his strength. His chin sank, and his voice when he spoke again was the voice of a weak and weary man.

"I talk.... I talk.... And then a desolating sense of reality blows like a destroying gust through my mind, and my little lamp of hope goes out....

"It is as if some great adversary sat over all my world, mocking me in every phrase I use and every act I do...."

He sighed deeply.

"Have I answered your questions, doctor!" he asked.

§ 6

"Yon speak of God," said Dr. Barrack. "But this that you speak of as God, is it really what men understand by God? It seems to me, as I said to begin with, it is just a personification of the good will in us all. Why bring in God? God is a word that has become associated with all sorts of black and cruel things. It sets one thinking of priesthoods, orthodoxies, persecutions. Why do you not call this upward and onward power Humanity? Why do you not call it the Spirit of Men? Then it might be possible for an Agnostic like myself to feel a sort of agreement...."

"Because I have already shown you it is not humanity, it is not the spirit of men. Humanity, the spirit of men, made poison gas and the submarine; the spirit of man is jealous, aggressive and partisan. Humanity has greed and competition in grain, and the spirit of man is fear and hatred, secrecy and conspiracy, quite as much as, much more than, it is making or order. But this spirit in me, this fire which I call God, was lit, I know not how, but as if it came from outside....

"I use the phrases," said Mr. Huss, "that come ready to the mind. But I will meet you so far as to say that I know that I am metaphorical and inexact.... This spirit that comes into life—it is more like a person than a thing and so I call it He. And He is not a feature, not an aspect of things, but a selection among things.... He seizes upon and brings out and confirms all that is generous in the natural impulses of the mind. He condemns cruelty and all evil....

"I will not pretend to explain what I cannot explain. It may be that God is as yet only foreshadowed in life. You may reason, Doctor Barrack, that this fire in the heart that I call God, is as much the outcome of your Process as all the other things in life. I cannot argue against that. What I am telling you now is not what I believe so much as what I feel. To me it seems that the creative desire that burns in me is a thing different in its nature from the blind Process of matter, is a force running contrariwise to the power of confusion.... But this I do know, that once it is lit in a man it is like a consuming fire. Once it is lit in a man, then his mind is alight— thenceforth. It rules his conscience with compelling power. It summons him to live the residue of his days working and fighting for the unity and release and triumph of mankind. He may be mean still, and cowardly and vile still, but he will know himself for what he is.... Some ancient phrases live marvellously. Within my heart *I know that my Redeemer liveth....*"

He stopped abruptly.

Dr. Barrack was unprepared with a reply. But he shook his head obstinately. These time-worn phrases were hateful to his soul. They smacked to him of hypocrisy, of a bidding for favour with obsolete and discredited influences. Through such leaks it is superstition comes soaking back into the laboriously bailed-out minds of men. Yet Mr. Huss was a difficult controversialist to grapple. "No," said the doctor provisionally. *"No...."*

§ 7

Fate came to the relief of Dr. Barrack.

The little conference at Sea View was pervaded by the sense of a new personality. This was a short and angry and heated little man, with active dark brown eyes in a tan face, a tooth-brush moustache of iron-grey, and a protruded lower jaw. He was dressed in a bright bluish-grey suit and bright brown boots, and he carried a bright brown leather bag.

He appeared mouthing outside the window, beyond the

range of distinct hearing. His expression was blasphemous. He made threatening movements with his bag.

"Good God!" cried Dr. Barrack. "Sir Alpheus!... I had no idea of the time!"

He rushed out of the room and there was a scuffle in the passage.

"I ought to have been met," said Sir Alpheus, entering, " I ought to have been met. It's ridiculous to pretend you didn't know the time. A general practitioner *always* knows the time. It is his first duty. I cannot understand the incivility of this reception. I have had to make my way to your surgery, Dr. Barrack, without assistance; not a cab free at the station; I have had to come down this road in the heat, carrying everything myself, reading all the names on the gates— the most ridiculous and banal names. The Taj, Thyme Bank, The Cedars, and Capernaum, cheek by jowl! It's worse than Freud."

Dr. Barrack expressed further regrets confusedly and indistinctly.

"We have been talking. Sir Alpheus," said Sir Eliphaz, advancing as if to protect the doctor from his specialist, "upon some very absorbing topics. That must be our excuse for this neglect. We have been discussing education— and the universe. Fate, free-will, predestination absolute." It is not every building contractor can quote Milton.

The great surgeon regarded the patentee of Temanite.

"Fate— fiddlesticks!" said Sir Alpheus suddenly and rudely. "That's no excuse for not meeting me." His bright little eyes darted round the company and recognized Mr. Huss. "What! my patient not in bed! Not even in bed! Go to *bed*, sir! Go to *bed*!"

He became extremely abusive to Dr. Barrack. "You treat an operation, Sir, with a levity—!"

VI. — THE OPERATION

§ 1

WHILE Sir Alpheus grumbled loudly at the unpreparedness of everything, Mr. Huss, with the assistance of Dr. Barrack, walked upstairs and disrobed himself.

This long discussion had taken a very powerful grip upon his mind. Much remained uncertain in his thoughts. He had still a number of things he wanted to say, and these proceedings preliminary to his vivisection, seemed to him to be irrelevant and tiresome rites interrupting something far more important.

The bed, the instruments, the preparation for anaesthesia, were to him no more than new contributions to the argument. While he lay on the bed with Dr. Barrack handling the funnel hood that was to go over nose and mouth for the administration of the chloroform, he tried to point out that the very idea of operative surgery was opposed to the scientific fatalism of that gentleman. But Sir Alpheus interrupted him....

"Breathe deeply," said Dr. Barrack....

"Breathe deeply...."

The whole vast argumentative fabric that had arisen in his mind swung with him across an abyss of dread and mental inanity. Whether he thought or dreamt what follows it is impossible to say; we can but record the ideas that, like a crystalline bubble as great as all things, filled his consciousness.

He felt a characteristic doubt whether the chloroform would do its duty, and then came that twang like the breaking of a violin string:— *Ploot*....

And still he did not seem to be insensible! He was not insensible, and yet things had changed. Dr. Elihu was still present, but somehow Sir Eliphaz and Mr. Dad and Mr. Farr, whom he had left downstairs, had come back and were sitting on the ground— on the ashes; they were all seated gravely on a mound of ashes and beneath a sky that blazed with light. Sir Alpheus, the nurse, the bedroom, had vanished. It seemed that they had been the dream.

But this was the reality, an enduring reality, this sackcloth and these reeking ash-heaps outside the city gates. This was the scene of an unending experiment and an immortal argument. He was Job; the same Job who had sat here for thousands of years, and this lean vulturous old man in the vast green turban was Eliphaz the Temanite, the smaller man who peered out of the cowl of a kind of hooded shawl, was his friend Bildad the Shuhite; the eager, coarse face of the man in unclean linen was Zophar the Naamathite; and this fist-faced younger man who sat with an air of false humility insolently judging them all, was Elihu the son of Barachel the Buzite of the kindred of Earn....

It was queer that there should have ever been the fancy that these men were doctors or schoolmasters or munition makers, a queer veiling of their immortal quality in the transitory garments of a period. For ages they had sat here and disputed, and for ages they had still to sit. A little way off waited the asses and camels and slaves of the three emirs, and the two Ethiopian slaves of Eliphaz had been coming towards them bearing bowls of fine grey ashes. (For Eliphaz for sanitary reasons did not use the common ashes of the midden upon his head.) There, far away, splashed green with palms and pierced between pylons by a glittering arm of the river, were the low brown walls of sun-dried brick, the flat-roofed houses, and the twisted temple towers of the ancient city of Uz, where first this great argument had begun. East and west and north and south stretched the wide levels of the world, dotted with small date trees, and above them was the measureless dome of heaven, set with suns and stars and flooded with a light.

This light had shone out since Elihu had spoken, and it was not only a light but a voice clear and luminous, before which Job's very soul bowed and was still....

"Who is this that darkeneth counsel by words without knowledge?"

By a great effort Job lifted up his eyes to the zenith.

It was as if one shone there who was all, and yet who comprehended powers and kingdoms, and it was as if a screen or shadow was before his face. It was as if a dark figure enhaloed in shapes and colours bent down over the whole world and regarded it curiously and malevolently, and it was as if this dark figure was no more than a translucent veil before an infinite and lasting radiance. Was it a veil before the light, or did it not rather nest in the very heart of the light and spread itself out before the face of the light and spread itself and recede and again expand in a perpetual diastole and systole? It was as if the voice that spoke was the voice of God, and yet ever and again it was as if the timbre of the voice was Satan. As the voice spoke to Job, his friends listened and watched him, and the eyes of Elihu shone like garnets and the eyes of Eliphaz like emeralds, but the eyes of Bildad were black like the eyes of a lizard upon a wall, and Zophar had no eyes but looked at him only with the dark shadows beneath his knitted brows. As God spake they all, and Job with them, became smaller and smaller and shrank until they were the minutest of conceivable things, until the whole scene was a little toy; they became unreal like discolourations upon a floating falling disc of paper confetti, amidst greatnesses unfathomable.

"Who is this that darkeneth counsel by words without knowledge?"

But in this dream that was dreamt by Mr. Huss while he was under the anaesthetic, God did not speak by words but by light; there were no sounds in his ears, but thoughts ran like swift rivulets of fire through his brain and gathered into pools and made a throbbing pattern of wavelets, curve within curve, that interlaced....

The thoughts that it seemed to him that God was speaking through his mind, can be put into words only after a certain fashion and with great loss, for they were thoughts about things beyond and above this world, and our words are all made out of the names of things and feelings in this world. Things that were contradictory had become compatible, and things incomprehensible seemed straightforward, because he was in a dream. It was as if the anaesthetic had released his ideas from their anchorage to words and phrases and their gravitation towards sensible realities. But it was still the same line of thought he pursued through the stars and spaces, that he had pursued in the stuffy little room at Sundering-on-Sea.

It was somewhat after this fashion that things ran through the mind of Mr. Huss. It seemed to him at first that he was answering the challenge of the voice that filled the world, not of his own will but mechanically. He was saying: "They*give* me knowledge."

To which the answer was in the voice of Satan and in tones of mockery. For Satan had become very close and definite to Job, as a dark face, time-worn and yet animated, that sent out circle after circle of glowing colour towards the bounds of space as a swimmer sends waves towards the bank. "But what have you got in the way of a vessel to hold your knowledge if we gave it you?"

"In the name of the God in my heart," said Job, " I demand knowledge and power."

"Who are yon! A pedagogue who gives ill-prepared lessons about history in frowsty rooms, and dreams that he has been training his young gentlemen to play leap-frog amidst the stars."

"I am Man," said Job.

"Huss."

But that queer power of slipping one's identity and losing oneself altogether which dreams will give, had come upon Mr. Huss. He answered with absolute conviction: " I am Man. Down there I was Huss, but here I am Man. I am every man who has ever looked up towards this light of God. I am every one who has thought or worked or willed for the race. I am all the explorers and leaders and teachers that man has ever had."

The argument evaporated. He carried his point as such points are carried in dreams. The discussion slipped to another of the issues that had been troubling him.

"You would plumb the deep of knowledge; you would scale the heights of space.... There is no limit to either."

"Then I will plumb and scale for ever. I will defeat you."

"But you will never destroy me."

"I will fight my way through you to God."

"And never attain him...."

It seemed as though yet another voice was speaking. For a while the veil of Satan was drawn aside. The thoughts it uttered ran like incandescent molten metal through the mind of Job, but whether he was saying these things to God or whether God was saying these things to him, did not in any way appear.

"So life goes on for ever. And in no other way could it go on. In no other way could there be such a being as life. For how can you struggle if there is a certainty of victory! Why should you struggle if the end is assured! How can you rise if there is no depths into which you can fall? The blacknesses and the evils about you are the warrants of reality....

"Through the centuries the voice of Job had complained and will complain. Through the centuries the fire of his faith flares and flickers and threatens to go out. But is Job justified in his complaints?

"Is Job indeed justified in his complaints? His mind has been coloured by the colour of misfortune. He has seen all the world reflecting the sufferings of his body. He has dwelt upon illness and cruelty and death. But is there any evil or cruelty or suffering that is beyond the possibility of human control? Were that so then indeed he might complain that God has mocked him.... Are sunsets ugly and oppressive? Do mountains disgust, do distant hills repel? Is there any flaw in the starry sky? If the lives of beasts and men are dark and ungracious, yet is not the texture of their bodies lovely beyond comparison? You have sneered because the beauty of cell and tissue may build up an idiot. Why, oh Man, do they build up an idiot? Have you no will, have you no understanding, that you suffer such things to be I The darkness and ungraciousness, the evil and the cruelty, are no more than a challenge to you. In you lies the power to rule all these things...."

Through the tumbled clouds of his mind broke the sunlight of this phrase: "The power to rule all these things. The power to rule—"

"You have dwelt overmuch upon pain. Pain is a swift distress; it ends and is forgotten. Without memory and fear pain is nothing, a contradiction to be heeded, a warning to be taken. Without pain what would life become? Pain is the master only of craven men. It is in man's power to rule it. It is in man's power to rule all things...."

It was as if the dreaming patient debated these ideas with himself; and again it was as if he were the universal all and Job and Satan and God disputed together within him. The thoughts in his mind raced faster and suddenly grew bright and glittering, as the waters grow bright when they come racing out of the caves at Han into the light of day. Green-faced, he murmured and stirred in his great debate while the busy specialist plied his scalpels, and Dr. Barrack whispered directions to the intent nurse.

"Another whiff," said Doctor Barrack.

"A cloud rolls back from my soul...."

"I have been through great darkness. I have been through deep waters...."

"Has not your life had laughter in it? Has the freshness of the summer morning never poured joy through your being? Do you know nothing of the embrace of the lover, cheek to cheek or lip to lip? Have you never swum out into the sunlit sea or shouted on a mountain slope? Is there no joy in a handclasp? Your son, your son, you say, is dead with honour. Is there no joy in that honour? Clean and straight was your son, and beautiful in his life. Is that nothing to thank God for? Have you never played with happy children? Has no boy ever answered to your teaching giving back more than you gave him? Dare you deny the joy of your appetites: the first mouthful of roast red beef on the frosty day and the deep draught of good ale? Do you know nothing of the task well done, nor of sleep after a day of toil? Is there no joy for the farmer in the red ploughed fields, and the fields shooting with green blades ? When the great prows smite the waves and the aeroplane hums in the sky, is man still a hopeless creature? Can you watch the beat and swing of machinery and still despair? Your illness has coloured the world; a little season of misfortune has hidden the light from your eyes."

It was as if the dreamer pushed his way through the outskirts of a great forest and approached the open, but it was not through trees that he thrust his way but through bars and nets and interlacing curves of blinding, many- coloured light towards the clear promise beyond. He had grown now to an incredible vastness so that it was no longer earth upon which he set his feet but that crystalline pavement whose translucent depths contain the stars. Yet though he approached the open he never reached the open; the iridescent net that had seemed to grow thin, grew dense again; he was still struggling, and the black doubts that had lifted for a moment swept down upon his soul again. And he realized he was in a dream, a dream that was drawing swiftly now to its close.

"Oh God!" he cried, "answer me! For Satan has mocked me

sorely. Answer me before I lose sight of you again. An) I right to fight? Am I right to come out of my little earth, here above the stars?"

"Right if you dare."

"Shall I conquer and prevail? Give me your promise!"

"Everlastingly you may conquer and find fresh worlds to conquer."

"*May*— but *shall* I?"

It was as if the torrent of molten thoughts stopped suddenly. It was as if everything stopped.

"Answer me," he cried.

Slowly the shining thoughts moved on again.

"So long as your courage endures you will conquer....

"If you have courage, although the night be dark, although the present battle be bloody and cruel and end in a strange and evil fashion, nevertheless victory shall be yours— in a way you will understand— when victory comes. Only have courage. On the courage in your heart all things depend. By courage it is that the stars continue in their courses, day by day. It is the courage of life alone that keeps sky and earth apart.... If that courage fail, if that sacred fire go out, then all things fail and all things go out, all things good and evil, space and time."

"Leaving nothing?"

"Nothing."

"Nothing," he echoed, and the word spread like a dark and darkening mask across the face of all things.

And then as if to mark the meaning of the word, it seemed to him that the whole universe began to move inward upon itself, faster and faster, until at last with an incredible haste it rushed together. He resisted this collapse in vain, and with a sense of overwhelmed effort. The white light of God and the whirling colours of the universe, the spaces between the stars— it was as if an unseen fist gripped them together. They rushed to one point as water in a clepsydra rushes to its hole. The whole universe became small, became a little thing, diminished to the size of a coin, of a spot, of a pinpoint, of one intense black mathematical point, and— vanished. He heard his own voice crying in the void like a little thing blown before the wind: "But will my courage endure?" The question went unanswered. Not only the things of space but the things of time swept together into nothingness. The last moment of his dream rushed towards the first, crumpled all the intervening moments together and made them one. It seemed to Mr. Huss that he was still in the instant of insensibility. That sound of the breaking string was still in his ears:— *Ploot....*

It became part of that same sound which came before the vision....

He was aware of a new pain within him; not that dull aching now, but a pain keen and sore. He gave a fluttering gasp.

"Quick," said a voice. "He is coming to!"

"He'll not wake for hours," said a second voice.

"His mouth and eyes!"

He lifted his eyelids as one lifts lead. He found himself looking into the intelligent but unsympathetic face of Sir Alpheus Mengo, he tried to comprehend his situation but he had forgotten how he got to it, he closed his eyes and sank back consciously and wilfully towards insensibility....

VII. — LETTERS AND A TELEGRAM

§ 1

IT was three weeks later.

Never had there been so successful an operation as an operation in the experience of either Sir Alpheus Mengo or Dr. Barrack. The growth that had been removed was a non-malignant growth; the diagnosis of cancer had been unsound. Mr. Huss was still lying flat in his bed in Mrs. Croome's house, but he was already able to read books, letters and newspapers, and take an interest in affairs.

The removal of his morbid growth had made a very great change in his mental atmosphere. He no longer had the same sense of an invisible hostile power brooding over all his life; his natural courage had returned. And the world which had seemed a conspiracy of misfortunes was now a hopeful world again. The last great offensive of the Germans towards Paris had collapsed disastrously under the counter attacks of Marshal Foch; each morning's paper told of fresh victories for the Allies, and the dark shadow of a German Caesarism fell no longer across the future. The imaginations of men were passing through a phase of reasonableness and generosity; the idea of an organized world peace had seized upon a multitude of minds; there was now a prospect of a new and better age such as would have seemed incredible in the weeks when the illness of Mr. Huss began to bear him down. And it was not simply a general relief that had come to his forebodings. His financial position, for example, which had been wrecked by one accident, had been restored by another. A distant cousin of Mr. Huss, to whom however Mr. Huss was the nearest relative, had died of softening of the brain, after a career of almost imbecile speculation. He had left his property partly to Mr. Huss and partly to Woldingstanton School. For some years before the war he had indulged in the wildest buying of depreciated copper shares, and had accumulated piles of what had seemed at the time valueless paper. The war had changed all that. Instead of being almost insolvent, the deceased in spite of heavy losses on Canadian land deals was found by his executors to be worth nearly thirty thousand pounds. It is easy to underrate the good in money. The windfall meant a hundred needed comforts and freedoms, and a release for the mind of Mrs. Huss that nothing else could have given her. And the mind of Mr. Huss reflected the moods of his wife much more than he suspected.

But still better things seemed to be afoot in the world of Mr. Huss. The rest of the governors of Woldingstanton, it became apparent, were not in agreement with Sir Eliphaz and Mr. Dad upon the project of replacing Mr. Huss by Mr. Farr; and a number of the old boys of the school at the front, getting wind of what was going on, had formed a small committee for the express purpose of defending their old master. At the head of this committee, by a happy chance, was young Kenneth Burrows, the nephew and heir of Sir Eliphaz. At the school he had never been in the front rank; he had been one of those good-all-round boys who end as a school prefect, a sound man in the first eleven, and second or third in most of the subjects he took. Never had he played a star part or enjoyed very much of the head's confidences. It was all the more delightful therefore to find him the most passionate and indefatigable champion of the order of things that Mr. Huss had set up. He had heard of the proposed changes at his uncle's dinner-table when on leave, and he had done something forthwith to shake that gentleman's resolves. Lady Burrows, who adored him, became at once pro-Huss. She was all the readier to do this because she did not like Mr. Dad's rather emphatic table manners, nor Mr. Farr's clothes.

"You don't know what Mr. Huss was to us, Sir," the young man repeated several times, and returned to France with that sentence growing and flowering in his mind. He was one of those good types for whom the war was a powerful developer. Death, hardship, and responsibility— he was still not two-and-twenty, and a major in the artillery— had already made an understanding man out of the schoolboy; he could imagine what dispossession meant; his new maturity made it seem a natural thing to write to comfort his old head as one man writes to another. His pencilled sheets, when first they came, made the enfeebled recipient cry, not with misery but happiness. They were re-read like a love-letter; they were now on the coverlet, and Mr. Huss was staring at the ceiling and already planning a new Woldingstanton rising from its ashes, greater than the old.

§ 2

It is only in the last few weeks, the young man wrote, *that we have heard of all these schemes to break up the tradition of*

153

Woldingstanton, and now there is a talk of your resigning the headmaster ship in favour of Mr. Farr. Personally, Sir, I can't imagine how you can possibly dream of giving up your work and to him of all people;— I still have a sort of doubt about it; but my uncle was very positive that you were disposed to resign (personally, he said, he had implored you to stay), and it is on the off-chance of his being right that I am bothering you with this letter. Briefly it is to implore you to stand by the school, which is as much as to say to stand by yourself and us. You've taught hundreds of us to stick it, and now you owe it to us to stick it yourself. I know you're ill, dreadfully ill; I've heard about Gilbert, and I know, Sir, we all know, although he wasn't in the school and you never betrayed a preference or were led into an unfair thing through it, how much you loved him; you've been put through it, Sir, to the last degree. But, Sir, there are some of us here who feel almost as though they were your sons; if you don't and can't give us that sort of love, it doesn't alter the fact that there are men out here who think of you as they'd like to think of their fathers. Men like myself particularly, who were left as boys without a father.

I'm no great hand at expressing myself; I'm no credit to Mr. Cross and his English class; generally I don't believe in saying too much; but I would like to tell you something of what you have been to a lot of us, and why Woldingstanton going on will seem to us like a flag still flying and Woldingstanton breaking its tradition like a sort of surrender. And I don't want a bit to flatter you, Sir, if you'll forgive me, and set you up in what I am writing to you. One of the loveable things about you to us is that you have always been so jolly human to us. You've always been unequal. I've seen you give lessons that were among the best lessons in the world, and I've seen you give some jolly bad lessons. And there

were some affairs—that business of the November fireworks for
example when we thought you were harsh and wrong—

"I was wrong," said Mr. Huss.

That almost led to a mutiny. But that is just where you score,
and why Woldingstanton can't do without you. When that
firework row was on we called a meeting of the school and house
prefects and had up some of the louts to it— you never heard of
that meeting— and we said, we all agreed you were wrong and
we all agreed that right or wrong we stood by you, and wouldn't
let the row go further. Perhaps you remember how that affair shut
up all at once. But that is where you've got us. You do wrong, you
let us see through you; there never was a schoolmaster or a father
gave himself away so freely as you do, you never put up a sham
front on us and consequently every one of us knows that what
he knows about you is the real thing in you; the very kids in the
lower fifth can get a glimpse of it and grasp that you are driving
at something with all your heart and soul, and that the school
goes somewhere and has life in it. We Woldingstanton boys have
that in common when we meet; we understand one another;
we have something that a lot of the other chaps one meets out
here, even from the crack schools, don't seem to have. It isn't a
'flourish with us, Sir, it is a simple statement of fact that the life
we joined up to at Woldingstanton is more important to us than
the life in our bodies. Just as it is more important to you. It isn't
only the way you taught it, though you taught it splendidly, it is
the way you felt it that got hold of us. You made us think and
feel that the past of the world was our own history; you made
us feel that we were in one living story with the reindeer men
and the Egyptian priests, with the soldiers of Caesar and the
alchemists of Spain; nothing was dead and nothing alien; you

made discovery and civilization our adventure and the whole future our inheritance. *Most of the men I meet here feel lost in this war; they are like rabbits washed out of their burrows by a flood, but we of Woldingstanton have taken it in the day's work, and when the peace comes and the new world begins, it will still be in the story for us, the day's work will still join on. That's the essence of Woldingstanton, that it puts you on the high road that goes on. The other chaps I talk to here from other schools seem to be on no road at all. They are tough and plucky by nature and association; they are fighters and sturdy men; but what holds them in it is either just habit and the example of people about them or something unsound that can't hold out to the end; a vague loyalty to the Empire or a desire to punish the Hun or restore the peace of Europe, some short range view of that sort, motives that will leave them stranded at the end of the war, anyhow, with nothing to go on to. To talk of after the war to them is to realise what blind alleys their teachers have led them into. They can understand fighting against things but not for things. Beyond an impossible ambition to go back somewhere and settle down us they used to be, there's not the ghost of an idea to them at all. The whole value of Woldingstanton is that it steers a man through and among the blind alleys and sets him on a way out that he can follow for all the rest of his days; it makes him a player in a limitless team and one with the Creator. We are all coming back to take up our jobs in that spirit, jobs that will all join up at last in making a real world state, a world civilization and a new order of things, and unless we can think of you, sir, away at Woldingstanton, working away to make more of us, ready to pick up the sons we shall send you presently—*

Mr. Huss stopped reading.

§ 3

He lay thinking idly.

"I was talking about blind alleys the other day. Queer that he should have hit on the same phrase....

"Some old sermon of mine perhaps.... No doubt I've had the thought before....

"I suppose that one could define education as the lifting of minds out of blind alleys....

"A permissible definition anyhow....

"I wish I could remember that talk better. I said a lot of things about submarines. I said something about the whole world really being like the crew of a submarine....

"It's true— universally. Everyone is in a blind alley until we pierce a road....

"That was a queer talk we had.... I remember I wouldn't go to bed— a kind of fever in the mind....

"Then there was a dream.

"I wish I could remember more of that dream. It was as if I could see round some metaphysical corner.... I seemed to be in a great place— talking to God....

"But how could one have talked to God?...

"No. It is gone...."

His thought reverted to the letter of young Burrows.

He began to scheme out the reinstatement of Woldingstanton. He had an idea of rebuilding School House with a map corridor to join it to the picture gallery and the concert hall, which were both happily still standing. He wanted the maps on one side to show the growth and succession of empires in the western world, and on the other to present the range of geographical knowledge and thought at different periods in man's history.

As with many great headmasters, his idle day-dreams were often architectural. He took out another of his dream toys now and played with it. This dream was that he could organize a series of ethnological exhibits showing various groups of primitive peoples in a triple order; first little models of them in their savage state, then displays of their arts and manufactures to show their distinctive gifts and aptitudes, and then suggestions of the part such a people might play as artists or guides, or beast tamers or the like, in a wholly civilized world. Such a collection would be far beyond the vastest possibilities to which Woldingstanton would ever attain—but he loved the dream.

The groups would stand in well-lit bays, side chapels, so to speak, in his museum building. There would be a group of seats and a blackboard, for it was one of his fantasies to have a school so great that the classes would move about it, like little groups of pilgrims in a cathedral....

From that he drifted to a scheme for grouping great schools for such common purposes as the educational development of the cinematograph, a central reference library, and the like....

For one great school leads to another. Schools are living things, and like all living things they must grow and reproduce their kind and go on from conquest to conquest— or fall under the sway of the Farrs and Dads and stagnate, become diseased and malignant, and perish. But Woldingstanton was not to perish. It was to spread. It was to call to its kind across the Atlantic and throughout the world.... It was to give and receive ideas, interbreed, and develop....

Across the blue October sky the white clouds drifted, and

the air was full of the hum of a passing aeroplane. The chained dog that had once tortured the sick nerves of Mr. Huss now barked unheeded.

"I would like to give one of the chapels of the races to the memory of Gilbert, " whispered Mr. Huss.

§ 4

The door at the foot of his bed opened, and Mrs. Huss appeared.

She had an effect of appearing suddenly, and yet she moved slowly into the room, clutching a crumpled bit of paper in her hand. Her face had undergone some extraordinary change; it was dead white, and her eyes were wide open and very bright. She stood stiffly. She might have been about to fall. She did not attempt to close the door behind her.

Mrs. Croome became audible rattling her pans downstairs.

When Mrs. Huss spoke, it was in an almost noiseless whisper. *"Job!"*

He had a strange idea that Mrs. Croome must have given them notice to quit instantly or perpetrated some such brutality, a suspicion which his wife's gesture seemed to confirm. She was shaking the crumpled scrap of paper in an absurd manner. He frowned in a gust of impatience.

"I didn't open it," she said at last, " not till I had eaten some breakfast. I didn't dare. I saw it was from the bank and I thought it might

be about the overdraft..... All the while.

She was weeping. "All the while I was eating my egg...."

"Oh *what* is it?"

She grimaced.

"From *him*."

He stared.

"A cheque, Job— come through— from *him*. From our boy."

His mouth fell open, he drew a deep breath. His tears came. He raised himself, and was reminded of his bandaged state and dropped back again. He held out his lean hand to her.

"He's a prisoner?" he gasped. "*Alive?*"

She nodded. She seemed about to fling herself violently upon his poor crumpled body. Her arms waved about seeking for something to embrace.

Then she flopped down in the narrow space between bed and paper-adorned fireplace, and gathered the counterpane together into a lump with her clutching hands. "Oh my baby boy"! she wept. *"My baby boy....*

"And I was so wicked about the mourning.... I was so *wicked...."*

Mr. Huss lay stiff, as the doctor had ordered to do; but the hand he stretched down could just touch and caress her hair.

THE END

A List of H. G Wells Books in this Series

FICTION

A Modern Utopia

Babes in the Darkling Wood - A Novel of Ideas

Boon, The Mind of the Race, The Wild Asses of the Devil, and The Last Trump

In the Days of the Comet

Kipps: The Story of a Simple Soul

Men Like Gods

Star-Begotten - A Biological Fantasia

The Autocracy of Mr. Parham - His Remarkable Adventures in This Changing World

The BrothersThe Camford Visitation

The Croquet Player

The Dream

The Fight in the Lion's Thicket

The First Horseman

The First Men in the Moon

The Grisly Folk

The Holy Terror

The Invisible Man

The King Who Was a King - The Book of a Film

The Land Ironclads

The New Machiavelli

The Passionate Friends

The Pearl of Love

The Queer Story of Brownlow's Newspaper

The Red Room

The Reign of Uya the Lion

The Research Magnificent

The Sea Lady

The Secret Places of the Heart

The Shape of Things to Come

The Sleeper Awakes - A Revised Edition of When the Sleeper Wakes

The Soul of a Bishop

The Time Machine

The Undying Fire

The War in the Air

The War of the Worlds

The Wife of Sir Isaac Harman

The Wild Asses of the Devil

The Wonderful Visit

The World Set Free

Ugh-Lomi and the Cave Bear

Ugh-Lomi and Uya

When the Sleeper Wakes

You Can't Be Too Careful

FICTION COLLECTIONS

The Short Stories of H. G. Wells

Tales of Space and Time

The Country of the Blind, and Others

The Door in the Wall, and Others

The Plattner Story and Others

The Stolen Bacillus and Others

The Time Machine and Others

Twelve Stories and a Dream

NON-FICTION

A Year of Prophesying

Anticipations

Certain Personal Matters

Crux Ansata

Experiment in Autobiography

First and Last Things: A Confession of Faith and Rule of Life

God, the Invisible King

Mankind in the Making

Marxism vs. Liberalism - An Interview

Mr. Belloc Objects to "The Outline of History"

New Worlds For Old: A Plain Account of Modern Socialism

Scientific War

Select Conversations with an Uncle (Now Extinct) and Two Other Reminiscences

Socialism and the Family

Text Book of Biology, Part 1: Vertebrata

The Anatomy of Frustration

The Common Sense of War and Peace

The Discovery of the Future

The Elements of Reconstruction

The Future in America

The Idea of a League of Nations

The Salvaging of Civilization

The Story of a Great Schoolmaster

The War That Will End War

This Misery of Boots (1907)

War and the Future:

What is Coming? A Forecast of Things after the War

World Brain

Printed in Great Britain
by Amazon

62423842R00099